Heaven's Watch

Second Edition

By Vanessa Haney

Cover by Thomas Schroeder

ISBN: 978-1-963756-97-5

Dedication

Enormous thanks to those who enthusiastically made the time to read and comment on an early draft: Kelly (with a new job), Blanca (with a newborn), and Amanda (with surgery looming). Your friendship, support and suggestions are invaluable.

Mike, there's no way I can properly thank you for all that you do; however, I'm particularly grateful that you don't smother me in the middle of the night when I wake you by tapping in my Notes app.

Connor, kids want their parents to be proud of them but the reverse is also true. Your moral support means the world to me.

Also by Vanessa Haney

Heaven's Lost (Book 1)
Heaven's Watch (Book 2)
Heaven's Call (Book 3)
The Chuparosa Chronicles (Short Stories)
The Devil's Memories (Book 4)

Prologue

Her smooth, delicate features belied the fact, but Fiona Deane was an ugly woman. Thomas perched atop a pine tree near the edge of the trailer park where she lived and watched her leave the tiny market. The shop was run by the lonely trailer park manager with whom Thomas had learned the eldest Deane witch had a running feud.

From what Thomas could tell, the manager's only crime was excessive congeniality. He could understand that, but Fiona had taken it upon herself to dole out a punishment so hateful that even a callous creature like himself could sympathize with the man. Not that Thomas would do anything to stop her.

And not that the manager knew any of this; if he thought about it at all, he merely assumed he was amidst a run of somewhat bad luck. Fiona's relentless wave of inconvenient and slightly unpleasant hexes was designed to wear him down over time. She knew that depression waited within everyone for the right mix of chemicals and circumstances that would set it free to creep around and inflict anguish on even the most joyous of souls.

Thomas sneered down at her and thought to

himself that she was exactly the kind of witch the Christians feared. She was the kind who would steal children and kill crops just for fun. The kind who watched from the crowd while innocent women burned.

Her petite figure was still curvy at nearly eighty-five years old and her hair, though faded with cotton white strands running throughout, was still copper in color like her granddaughter's. Looking closely, he noticed that Laura Deane had inherited the upturned shape and vivid green of Fiona's eyes as well.

She'd purchased a box of crackers from the hapless market man who was just then attempting to wave off a sudden swarm of biting gnats. Gnats that he just happened to be allergic to.

Thomas knew that crackers meant soup. There was no food in Hell and he didn't require nourishment of that kind anyway, but since returning to the human realm, he could once again appreciate a good meal. He'd spent many hours watching her prepare various soups and stews. They were the perfect dishes for someone of her means and a big pot would last for days, tasting better and better over time.

The aroma wafted out of her trailer and into the trees, causing a rumble in his stomach but he pushed his hunger aside and refocused on completing his mission. He had to be cautious, quick and direct because a witch like that would most likely know how to poison an angel. She was no fool and he knew she'd already sensed his presence.

She'd long since abandoned any pretense of kindness or

thoughtfulness but for the sole purpose of manipulating those around her. Plaguing that insipid shopkeeper with gnats didn't give her any particular joy, but it comforted Fiona to know that she could still perform some of the most difficult magic. Her body might have been failing at last, but her power was as strong as ever.

She made her way through the dark lane with an imperious stomp. Most of the streetlights were broken in the trailer park community she called home and that suited her just fine. Vista Pines was a far cry from the ski resorts, log cabins, and luxury apartments she'd enjoyed most of her life, though. It was only recently that she'd found herself unable to relish the lifestyle that had been afforded to her in her youth by collecting money and favors from gullible men.

She'd never planned to reach an age so advanced that even the most ridiculous of them would no longer play her games. Refusing to act the infirm grandmother for their charity, she bitterly settled in to spend her final years looking down on her trailer park neighbors with rarely more than forty dollars in her purse.

Fiona would argue that it was not arrogance that landed her in a single wide with rotting floorboards and a perpetual puddle at the front steps. The story she told herself was that she'd simply had the misfortune of preying upon the cruelest and greediest men Flagstaff, Arizona had to offer.

On occasion, she wondered if perhaps she should have allowed Brona's father to stay with her a bit longer. He was a hard worker who at least cared about their child, but Fiona was not content with an astronomy professor's salary and nights spent on blankets in the forest looking up at the stars. It was after an attempt to cure the boredom of one such night that she found herself pregnant and married in the first place. It was a stupid mistake that nearly derailed all of her ambitions.

She was not one to look back wistfully, but lately found herself wondering more often what the pension was like for a retired university professor. Not that it mattered since he'd died fifteen years earlier. The local paper gushed about him being surrounded by his loving children at the time, but Fiona knew that his first born wasn't there. She'd convinced her daughter that he abandoned her and, though she never met him, Brona hated her father.

Fiona was more fractious than usual that night and gave her soup a rough stir, sloshing a fair amount out of the pot. She'd been at the school all day, searching for a solution to a new problem that could not be ignored. She hadn't found it, but she was close.

A certain type of young girl started college with not just intelligence but a desperate need to break free from the constraints of life. School provided those girls a temporary reprieve from parents, husbands, churches, and corporations waiting to press down on their freedom and desire.

They could both lose and find themselves within the institution and their curiosity and sense of adventure would never be sharper than during those years. Fiona needed six such girls for the ritual she'd designed.

She was not so prosaic a witch that she planned to drink their blood for youth, though she was not above that either, if she had thought it would be worth the trouble. Blood magic was dark and difficult to sustain and, worse yet, one needed a demon to perform it. Over the years she'd found demons to be unpleasant and untrustworthy and she quite literally didn't have the energy for their kind anymore.

The cunning magic she'd relied on for so long to trick men out of their money could not contend with the cancer growing in her bones and she needed the strength of those girls to work a healing spell.

It was that secret Thomas hoped would make his offer more attractive. He alighted from his tree just as she poked her head out the door, scowling at the mud puddle at the bottom of the steps. She'd felt him from inside and though her spine stiffened with alarm, she would not give him the satisfaction of showing her fear.

Rather, she sighed impatiently with her hands on her hips. "I know you've been watching me. What are ya, and what d'ya want?"

He noted that she once might have had a lovely brogue of some sort, but her speech had become mostly Americanized over the years. If there was ever a sweet lilt to her voice, age and bad habits had since turned it gravelly and thick.

She could hide her fear but not her surprise when he showed himself and pushed her inside the trailer. Closing the door behind them, he crossed his arms and leaned against it. "Your wards are strong, but few have the skill to keep me out."

He could not fully unfurl his wings in her puny space but fluffed them out enough that she understood who she was dealing with. "I'm a family friend in need of a favor."

She regained her composure and busied herself with the pot bubbling on the two-burner stovetop, grumbling, "I don't do favors for anyone, 'specially family."

To Thomas's delight, it was vegetable beef soup. He moved her out of the way, took the wooden spoon from her hand and dipped it in the pot. Blowing on it as he brought it to his mouth, he explained, "I'm not *asking* per se."

He opened each of her cabinets until he found a bowl and then ladled out some soup for himself while she stood gaping at him. "Once you get your little coven together," he said, "I know a place where healing spells work surprisingly well. In fact, I intend to move there myself once your disagreeable granddaughters cease their gatekeeping of my retirement plans."

Granddaughters? She shook her head. "I don't know anything about them. I haven't seen Brona in—"

"Brona is dead," he interrupted her and ripped the top off the box of crackers. "In case you care."

He waited for her to process the fact that her daughter had passed on, but he needn't have bothered.

She would not waste time on such things and instead demanded, "Where is this healing place?"

Thomas found himself shocked by how the family line had changed, and how dramatically his daughters differed from the hateful woman in front of him. Powerful and bothersome as they were, Laura and Sarah were not cold women and just then he felt a hint of compassion for them. It was not enough to change his mind, but he could admit that they were the kind of children he had hoped for in the early days. *Before the punishment.*

"There must be a lot of power in that place," Fiona prodded, "even more in those girls if they can keep *you* out. Besides, don't you already have the ultimate address?"

"I live on the wrong side of the tracks," he shrugged. "And life gets more difficult for me each time I run away from home. Right now, I am little more than a pain in the ass to the powers that be, but that will change soon and I want to have my forever home lined up when it does."

"Well, I dunno know what you could possibly want from me."

He leaned close to her as if spilling a great secret. "Even angels from my zip code cannot summon spirits. The one I want will provide enough of a distraction for me to make the necessary moving arrangements. I'll deal with the ensuing temper tantrums later. As payment for this service, you can follow me in with your girl squad and I'll show you the best place to heal."

"The spirit…which one?"

He crumbled the crackers into his bowl and shoveled in another bite. "I need Tromluí."

She drew an uneasy breath. That kind of summons would require a significant amount of energy, energy that she was loathe to expend under the circumstances, but she wasn't one to pass up an opportunity either.

Brona's children were apparently capable of strong magic that could be useful to her, especially if she played them against the angel. Fiona would think more about that later, but at the very least, she could capitalize on his desires and get her rent paid for the month.

"The supplies will cost money." She grumbled.

Thomas knew she already had everything she needed but dug in his coat pocket and threw a wad of bills on the counter. "I'll be back tomorrow."

"Tromluí won't play nice with 'em." She snatched up the money, barely concealing her smugness as she counted. "I assume you know what you're doing."

Chapter One

"Go! Go! Go!" Sebastian Scott charged over the hill waving his arms and shouting. The creature swooped over him and dove at Laura with its claws extended, poised to pluck out her eyes. It had the body of a vulture with the head of a woman. The feathers on top of which gave it a shabby, disheveled look. It emitted an enraged, high-pitched squawk as Laura turned and ran, covering her head with her hands.

As it gained on her, she stopped short and when it overshot, she flicked at the phosphorus paint on her fingernails to fill her palms with fire. The creature shrieked and cursed as she pushed out with her hands and engulfed it in flames.

On any other occasion, she might have felt guilty about killing something from the Other Side, especially a being she knew so little about. After catching sight of the deep, bloody gashes across Sebastian's shoulders though, she curled her lip at the writhing thing and hissed, "Burn, bitch."

She took Bash's wrist and slapped on his shield

bracelet. His skin tingled as the magnetic clasp connected and the protection of her magical armor flowed around his body. He'd lost it earlier and she found it hanging on a mesquite tree.

"Somehow I will make the shield permanent," she assured him.

"Shit. Baby, look at that." he pointed to the darkening sky behind them, then unholstered his pistol and spun the empty cylinder for her to see. "We're in trouble."

Her lips thinned. "They're harpies, Bash. I count eight."

"You can explain to me what a harpy is later." He took her hand, "Let's go."

They started down the hill as the raptors closed in on them from above. One managed to snatch Laura's ponytail, ripping out the elastic and dragging her backward until she reached up and grabbed its legs. Yanking it forward, she swung the squalling bird like a baseball bat against a Saguaro and threw the addled thing into a Creosote bush.

Hot desert wind blew the loose strands of hair across her face and as she filled her hands with fire once more, the fading light of the sunset gave her the appearance of an angry goddess. Watching his dangerous lover advance on the creature, Bash was overcome with a disturbing combination of anxiety and desire. She was furious that he was hurt, but he was fairly sure that harpy would stay down for a while and there were plenty more on the way.

"Leave it!" He shouted. They dropped onto their backsides, slid the rest of the way down the hill, and lurched toward her red Jeep parked below.

"I'll hold them off and you get us out of here!" She threw him the keys and steadied herself while sliding her upper body through the top rails on the passenger's side.

"Watson!" She scanned the area frantically for her dog.

The massive German Shepherd bounded around the base of the hill, followed by two large bobcats. They leapt and swatted at the vultures until Laura shouted, "Watson, get in here!"

The dog skidded into the back seat as Bash jammed his foot on the clutch and threw the Jeep into gear.

One of the Bobs leapt to the top of a boulder and took down a harpy as it plunged toward them. The vulture slashed and snapped, then stilled when the bobcat bit into its eerie, human looking face. Bile rose in Bash's throat. He shook his head to erase the image, released the clutch and floored the gas. The other creatures were closing in fast, so Laura flicked her fingernails and refilled her hands with fire.

"Keep your eyes open for Drew."

Earlier that week, the Sheriff's office had received three complaints in a row from hunters scouting the area ahead of dove season. Deputy Scott was told that turkey vultures were attacking the hunters, their dogs, and even their kids. Turkey vultures were strictly scavengers, so he knew something more troubling was on the loose and assumed it was from the Other Side. He and Laura never once considered harpies when they set out that afternoon.

Bash, Laura, and their friend Drew had driven deep

into the desert, hoping to find the source of the complaints. They came across some unusual markings that appeared to be a map made up of symbols and cairns. The map started at the edge of town and led deep into the mountains. They followed the symbols, intending to send whatever created the map back to the Other Side or, if it was unreasonable, send it somewhere more permanent.

Though it was not a well-coordinated attack, the harpies had swarmed them as soon as they arrived and the trio found themselves scattered and vulnerable. The creatures were extraordinarily defensive so Laura's group had obviously stumbled onto something they weren't supposed to see and she was disgusted with herself for not being more prepared.

Her mind reeled as they scrambled to get away. Ancient creatures like that tended to be uninterested in humans. They were typically unwilling to risk a trip through the veil, even as thin as it was in that area. She wondered if Thomas was involved, though he wasn't likely to bother with the Other Side after his last attempt at controlling them had failed so miserably. Even so, she warily looked around for him at every turn.

The harpies followed in a 'V' formation as Bash sped across the sand looking for their friend. The Jeep was fast and Laura was able to fight off the vultures individually with her magic, bringing their number to six. She couldn't hold them back indefinitely though, especially if Bash had to stop for an injured Drew.

As their eyes strained to find him in the darkness, an enormous mountain lion ran alongside the Jeep. Bash jumped in his seat at the sight of her, but he was relieved to have the extra help. If that was her intent.

"Adira!" he called out, "Where's Drew? Is he hurt?"

He felt her voice in his head, a sensation he would never truly be comfortable with. "Follow me, Sebastian."

She peeled off to the left, and Bash glanced at Laura. "Hold on, baby."

One of the harpies took advantage of the slowing vehicle as he downshifted to follow Adira, but Laura was ready, shooting a stream of fire into its breast. Its flaming body hit the bushes and she announced, "Five left."

Bash swore as they came upon Drew crouched in front of a large rock formation and firing on a wounded harpy as it shuffled toward him through the dirt. Drew had winged it with his pistol, a useless weapon against such a thing. They'd brought shotguns with them but hadn't had time to grab the weapons when they were attacked.

Bash slowed next to him. "Get in, god dammit!"

Drew jumped through the rails into the back of the Jeep but as Bash sped away, he lost his grip and slid across the seat into Watson, who snapped his jaws on Drew's collar, holding tight to keep the man inside the vehicle.

Drew ran his hands blindly across the floor of the Jeep until he found the twenty-gauge shot gun. Standing up through the rails, he racked the slide and blew a harpy out of the sky.

Bash backed off the accelerator and Drew and Laura jumped out of the Jeep. He put it in park, grabbed the other shotgun and they stood with their backs together as the four remaining harpies circled overhead. Watson growled and barked at Laura's side and she grew the flames in her hands. The sun had fully set by then so it was as much for them to see in the dark as it was to fight.

The creatures hovered too high in the sky for the shotguns to reach them, but Bash had an idea. He didn't know anything about harpies but he knew plenty about vultures. He handed Drew his gun and pulled his shirt over his head.

"What the hell are you doing?" Mystified at first, Drew understood the plan as soon as Bash revealed the ripped, bloody flesh across his back and shoulders. He took his shotgun back and laid it on the ground in front of him, then dramatically dropped to his knees in the dirt.

If Bash was right, the vultures would believe he was dying, or at least badly wounded and they wouldn't be able to resist him. For once, he hoped they would be attacked.

As soon as they saw him fall, the harpies dove at them all at once. "Your plan is working a little too well!" Drew yelled.

Laura screamed and threw a wall of fire between Bash and the raptors. In his head, he'd seen himself jumping up and blasting away at them, and though his knees would not cooperate with anything more than an awkward lunge, he *was* able to shoot through the flames and send them spiraling in all directions.

Laura swept her arms away from Bash and surrounded a harpy in a blanket of fire. Once finally on his feet, Bash racked and fired again, taking out another one. As Drew shot a third, Laura shouted for them to stop and the last harpy soared away, venting a stream of enraged curses in its wake.

Bash raised the shotgun to his shoulder again but she held his arm and said, "Let it go." Cupping her hands to her mouth, she yelled after it, "Tell your friends we are not fucking around!"

After staggering around in nervous circles for a while, they managed to catch their breath, but as they returned to the Jeep Bash put his arm around Laura's waist and collapsed against her. She and Drew eased him to the ground and pulled him forward to examine his back.

"I'm fine," he gasped.

She rained light, worried kisses across his face and he gave her hand a reassuring squeeze, repeating, "Baby, I'm fine."

The Bobs reappeared on either side of Drew, who absent-mindedly scratched their heads until Adira emerged from the shadows, ears flat and tail swishing. Sensing the annoyance of their mistress, they rubbed their backs against Drew's legs and then bounded off to the darkness.

Drew shook the dust off of Bash's shirt and handed it to him. "These little battles aren't so little anymore."

Adira tossed her head and her voice echoed through each of their minds. "This is only the beginning, and you are not strong enough to handle all that is coming your way."

* * *

"Harpies?" Deputy Chuck Ruiz snapped a pair of tongs in the air. "We're dealing with old school Greek shit now?"

Chuck's daughter, Tina, had just turned twenty and

they'd been on their way to her birthday party before the battle with the harpies. Bash had thought they could easily handle whatever was vexing the hunters before celebrating with the rest of their friends but as Drew said, it was nothing close to easy.

"I should have known better." He cursed himself for his arrogance. They dealt with it alright, but only just, and his little army staggered into Chuck's back yard exhausted, bedraggled and, once again, lucky to be alive. He flipped a bistro chair around and straddled it, adding, "Well, dove season ought to go a little bit smoother now."

Chuck was grilling long strips of marinated steak for carne asada and the scent of peppers, orange, and garlic made Bash's mouth water. It was when he rested his forehead on the back of the chair that Chuck noticed all the blood seeping through his friend's shredded henley shirt.

He put down his tongs and rubbed the back of Bash's head. "You okay, man?"

Laura and Chuck's wife, Mena, stepped outside with a dish of water for Watson and another to dress Bash's wounds. Laura's niece, Audi, and her boyfriend, Noah, followed. Noah was a paramedic and since meeting Audi's family he'd taken to carrying an extra trauma bag around with him.

He made a face at Bash's back. "Is this going to become a habit, Sheriff? Should I keep a separate kit with your name on it?"

"That's not a bad idea, son." Drew said, not joking at all.

He had been chatting with some of the guests by the pool, trying his best to keep them informed without causing a panic. To be fair, they'd burst into the backyard party, dirty and bleeding and he had to admit that he would have been the first one shouting questions if their positions were reversed.

Damage control wasn't really an option anymore, so he moved to help Bash out of the chair. "We should take this indoors."

Chuck stopped him and told Noah to get started. "We're all family here. They know what we do, and why. It doesn't hurt them to see what we're up against."

Bash looked up and gave Chuck's relatives a grim smile. He was grateful for their patience and their support but he felt bad for Tina. *What a birthday, poor kid.*

Tina Ruiz was a shy young woman who had negotiated as small a get together as her gregarious mother and large family would allow. As far as she was concerned, the less attention focused on her the better. She harbored an intense crush on Deputy Sheriff Sebastian Scott though, and worried for him that night. Since he was thirty years her senior, she had no real aspirations for his affection but allowed herself a heaving internal sigh whenever he swaggered around in that cowboy hat of his.

While Audi's Aunt Laura seemed considerably less impressed with his swagger, no one could question her love for him. In the past he'd been a bit reckless with Laura's heart and though Audi hadn't forgiven him for that, their relationship seemed to be everything Tina dreamed of for herself: dramatic, sexy, and strong.

Watson nudged at her hips as if to give her his birthday regards so she knelt to give him kisses and a bite of steak from her plate, grateful he wasn't hurt during the fight.

Sebastian bit down on the back of the chair and stifled a growl while Noah cleaned his back with antiseptic. Laura took his hand and gave it a squeeze. His eyes were red and tired, and his jaw was clenched in pain, but he was the most handsome man she'd ever seen in real life. She crouched to kiss his cheek and whisper as much into his ear.

He chuckled and squeezed back, tugging her close so only she could hear him say, "Move in with me."

She stood up straight and touched her hand to her throat. "What?"

"I know my timing sucks." He nudged her back down. "We'll talk more later—just think about it, okay?"

She gave him a stunned nod and a peck on the lips. "I will."

"Mom? What the hell is going on? Are you okay?"

Laura's son, Brian, came through the gate carrying a gift in one hand and a duffel bag over his shoulder. He and Tina were great friends and he'd arranged a ride down from NAU for her party.

Laura hugged him tight. "We ran into some trouble on the way over, but I'm fine."

"Was it Thomas?"

"No, there's a lot going on in town right now, honey. We're dealing with creatures we've never seen before. Thomas may have something to do with it, but I'm not sure. Anyway, Daniel warned us this would happen."

She spoke with the freedom of no longer having to shield him from the dangers they faced. He'd proven he could fight alongside them if necessary and while she would always worry, she could also count on his abilities to defend himself.

Drew caught Brian casting a glare at Bash and clapped him on the back. "Hey, let's get some food," he said, "How's school? You graduate in May, right?"

Brian gave his mother a troubled look as they headed to the food tables, so Drew tried to ease his mind. "Listen, your mom is the bravest woman I've ever known and the most powerful, too. Give her some credit, okay?"

Brian narrowed his eyes. "I know he gets her into trouble."

Drew shook his head. Brian's attitude toward Bash was understandable, to a point. It would only hurt them in the long run though, and he needed to be set straight, especially if he planned to come back to town after school. "No, sir. Sebastian takes the same risks she does and without the powers she has to protect himself."

Brian thought for a moment. "I guess you do, too."

Drew filled his plate with rice, tortillas, and strips of carne asada. "I recall you showing up for us a few months ago, so we're all in the same fight and we're all on the same team."

Brian took a plate from the stack. "Maybe."

"And Brian, he loves her."

Brian was unconvinced. "We'll see."

"They both have strong personalities and they fight but believe me when I say it's going to last. By the way, I thought you were bringing Olivia down this time to meet your mom."

Brian winced. "We broke up."

Drew put his plate down. "Brian, I'm sorry. Do you want to tell me what happened?"

He shrugged. "I didn't want to get her involved in

this mess."

Drew sighed. "The world is full of monsters of every kind, and you've got to trust that people can handle the truth. It's not good to isolate yourself like this."

"Yeah, but I'm one of the monsters."

"Brian..."

The young man put his hand up and argued, "Olivia is a scientist. That's her truth and I just let her off the hook is all. Now she can believe whatever she wants to."

Drew scratched the back of his head. "Did you protect her or did you leave her broken hearted and unprepared for the future?"

Brian hadn't thought about it that way, and he'd already fully burned the bridge. Olivia would never forgive him. He made sure of that, thinking it was for the best.

"Bash thought he was doing the right thing when he broke up with your mom. He knows it was a mistake and now they're back together and stronger than ever. He's made himself a target just to be with her, so do me a favor and don't judge him too harshly, especially if you're going to act just like him."

Brian did not like the comparison. "I thought you'd be on my side."

"I will always be on your side, but I'm gonna tell you when I think you're wrong. You're wrong about him and you're wrong about being a monster."

Laura left Bash in Noah's hands and texted her sister on the way to the bathroom:

L: Where are you?
S: With Rhonda—almost there.

Sarah had not been herself for months. Laura couldn't fathom losing a husband after thirty years, even if they didn't have the greatest marriage. The shock to Sarah's life was unimaginable, and she worried that the combination of grief and guilt had started her sister on something of a downward spiral.

Laura stopped short at the bathroom door and looked anxiously around the small room. She held her breath and threw open the shower curtain. Even though the tub was empty, her exhale came out in sharp, uneven gasps and she gripped the side of the sink to steady herself.

There was no demon impersonating her mother in the bathtub that night, but her mother was always present in her reflection. It was a remnant of the demon Laura would never be rid of. She took a washcloth from the shelf and rubbed at the dirt on her face.

"You're going to rub your whole face off, girl." Mena appeared in the doorway and took the cloth from her.

"Sometimes I think that wouldn't be so bad." Moisture brimmed her eyelids and she took the washcloth back, soaking it under the faucet. "Do you ever notice that those men get better looking all the time, and we just get…older?"

"Who's we?" Mena scoffed. "Not you, and not me." She smoothed Laura's hair back. "You drove that man to his colonoscopy, Laura." She raised her finger in the air. "There is no higher love, and he knows it. You've just gone through yet another major trauma out there and you're taking it out on yourself, as usual. You have got to develop better coping mechanisms. What the hell is a harpy, anyway?"

"He wants me to move in." Laura blurted. "He just asked me."

Mena took a step back. "Just now? Why is he springing this on you after everything that happened tonight? Does he ever think before he speaks?"

Laura chuckled. "He just got shredded by a mythological being so I'm not questioning his sense of urgency. In fact, on one hand I'm thrilled that he asked, but on the other I'm scared to death. Mena, I raised a man from scratch but I don't know how to live with one that's pre-made, out of the box."

"What are you talking about?"

"We're not a young couple starting out. I mean, at this age how do we figure out who pays for what? Who does the chores? I can't tell Sebastian that I'll knock him into next week if he doesn't pick his underwear up off the floor, like I used to tell Brian."

"Why not?"

"And since Brian left home, I'm practically feral. Do you know that sometimes I just eat cheese for dinner? Will I be expected to feed him every night?"

Mena laughed at her. "You're having a breakdown over this stupid stuff because you're afraid to bring up what really matters to you. You want a place for your son, and a place for the garden you've worked so hard on—the one you *need* for your business." Mena looked over the top of her glasses. "And you've got to admit that you're terrified of losing your hard-won independence. Why can't he move in with you?"

Laura wiped her face with the cool cloth. "His house is bigger and in much better shape, so it does make make more sense when you think about it. The logistics will be messy for me, but I want to do it. I guess I'm just overwhelmed. I didn't expect him to—"

"You didn't expect him to want you forever. When are you going to realize that you're worthy of love? Even if it's from that idiot. I swear to God, if there's a difficult way to do something, Sebastian Scott will find it."

Chapter Two

When Noah finished taking care of Bash, the two of them met Drew at a food table. Brian had since joined his friends by the pool and Drew was filling up a second plate.

"Near death experiences always make me so hungry," He said.

"Me, too." Laura stepped out of the patio door and handed Bash a fresh t-shirt and a beer.

"Woman, you spoil me."

She rested her head on his shoulder and looked up at him. "Are you okay?"

He stroked her cheek and winked at Noah. "My doctor says I'll live."

She gave him a doubtful look but filled a plate and left with Mena to chat with their kids.

"What happened here?" Noah poked at a long red scratch running the length of Drew's right arm.

Drew shoveled another spoonful of rice into his mouth and shrugged him off, nodding in the direction of the other young people across the yard.

"Not that we don't enjoy your company son, but aren't you at the wrong table?"

Noah hemmed and hawed for a bit, then shoved his hands in his pockets, turned to Bash, and asked, "Sheriff, how is it that you make Laura so happy? What's your secret?"

Chuck choked on his beer and Drew looked at the ground.

Bash gave his friends a wounded frown but acknowledged, "Happy is a strong word. Today was a pretty good day, though." *I think*, he added to himself. She hadn't given his invitation the enthusiastic response he'd hoped for, but she hadn't shut him down either, so he remained hopeful.

Noah held up the shredded shirt, then tossed it in the trash bin. "You call that a good day?"

Bash made a face. "For us, yes. Hell, kid, you don't have to make a woman happy—that's on her—just try not to make her sad." Noah furrowed his brow so Bash softened his tone, "You're gonna fuck it up but the right woman will appreciate that you're trying and she might even stick around."

Noah thought for a minute, then dropped a tube of antibiotic cream into Drew's hand. He made his way to where Audi reclined on a lounge chair with a bowl of tortilla chips in her lap and called over his shoulder, "Don't let that get infected."

Chuck laughed, "Poor kid. I wouldn't be twenty-five years old again for anything."

"I don't know," Bash grumbled and shifted uncomfortably on his feet while digging around for pain reliever in Noah's bag. "I would sure like my twenty-five-year-old body back."

Noah had been on the receiving end of an unhealthy dose of attitude from Audi all night and Drew felt bad for the younger man. It was in Audi's nature to put up walls anyway and he had no doubt that she felt more compelled lately to lash out while grieving the loss of her father. In his way Bash had given Noah some good advice and Drew felt that if he was patient, the couple might be able to make it work.

Contemplating the virtue of patience, he scanned the yard wondering if Sarah would bother to make an appearance at the party. He started for the beer cooler with a sigh, and then Chuck nudged his shoulder as she pushed open the gate.

Rhonda was with her and the older woman made her way through the small crowd offering hugs and hellos. She handed Mena's aunt a sinister looking bottle that caused Drew to instinctively place a hand over his belly. Rhonda had treated him when he nearly poisoned himself with tequila a few months earlier, but that cure was no fun.

Sarah lingered by the gate and took in the mellow party scene. She was wearing black skinny jeans and a short-sleeved, denim, button-up shirt that was unbuttoned enough to reveal some lace at the top of her bra. Her dark hair swung freely down her back and a large smokey quartz in the shape of a heart hung from a braided leather cord at her throat. The change in her appearance of late had been subtle, easily unnoticed by those who didn't know her well, but Drew noticed everything about her.

There were no more buns in her hair, extra buttons were left undone, and her jeans were tighter. He guessed that she was experimenting with looks that had made her uncomfortable in the past, or that Rueben had disapproved of.

She'd been married young to an older man and tried to compensate for her youth with a mature demeanor that hid her more whimsical, youngest child tendencies. Rueben was killed in the battle against Thomas and since then, Sarah was finding her way without him and rediscovering her true nature in the process.

Drew very much approved of her new look and of how her inhibitions had loosened. She grinned when she saw him and rushed to give him a big hug. She had taken to hugging everyone in those days, but did she cling a little longer to him that night? Or was he riled up from the battle with the harpies and letting his imagination act out his wishes?

Laura touched the quartz necklace Sarah wore and could feel the vibrations emanating from the crystal. That stone would absorb a fair amount of dark energy before it could permeate Sarah's psyche. It would be helpful to anyone who manifested its power but the angel magic Sarah worked into the leather cord was strong.

"Nice job."

Drew unconsciously reached for his wrist and twisted the bracelet that Laura made him. A bobcat had once bounced off its protective shield. If Laura was impressed with Sarah's fledgling spell work, he couldn't imagine the power held within that quartz necklace.

Laura let go of it and poured her sister a glass of sangria from the pitcher on a nearby table. "Not that I'm complaining, but since when do you care about spells?"

Sarah took a sip and her eyes widened. "This is good

and strong. Spells are more fun than I thought and apparently our survival is going to depend on them." She eased herself down to a patio chair next to where Laura was standing and started picking tiny spines from her sister's jeans. "These pants are trashed—good god, why do you have cactus in your butt?"

Laura gave Drew an exasperated look so he answered for her. "We've had a very long night."

He set about telling Sarah their story, so Laura found Bash by the pool sitting sideways on a chaise lounge. She sat on the deck between his legs, kicked off her shoes, and dangled her feet in the cool water. He guided her head to rest on his knee and combed through her hair with his fingers.

While other states get to celebrate a distinct fall season, summer lingers in Arizona well into October. It was late August then, and the hot, heavy air of the monsoon showed no sign of letting up.

Mena made Chuck install a misting system before the party and she'd decorated the back yard with luminarias and floated giant fake lily pads in the pool. The Ruiz house had an uninhibited view of the mountains and the moon rose over them creating a lovely, if sweltry scene.

They were bone tired but enjoying a well-deserved break with their friends. Chuck and Bash discussed a local ammo shortage, Mena gossiped to Laura about a handsome new park ranger spotted on the trails and the kids remained huddled by the diving board on the other side of the pool. Sarah was fixated on Drew as he told her all about the harpies in the mountains.

Just as Laura let her eyes flutter closed, a cold shiver ran down her spine and she jumped up, turning in circles while anxiously searching the yard for danger.

Bash followed her, instantly on full alert. "What is it, baby?"

Sarah stepped defensively in front of Drew when the gate swung open and Thomas sauntered in holding a small, gift-wrapped box and an oval shaped picture frame.

He bowed at the waist and handed the gift to Tina. "Happy birthday, Christina." Brian took it from her and set it on the ground as if it were a bomb.

"Traitor." Thomas snarled, referring to Brian's part in sending him back to Hell a few months earlier. "I would kill you right now, but I should have known you would never betray your mother. So, you get a pass." He raised a finger in the air. "Just the one."

Laura's phosphorous nails were ruined, so she swiped some flame from the top of a citronella candle and tossed a ball of fire between her hands as Thomas approached.

Eight of Chuck's relatives were still at the party, and seven were armed. This number included Chuck's mother-in-law who casually pulled a Colt Defender from her purse and aimed it at Thomas as he walked by.

Thomas was aware of his audience though and unfurled his enormous gray wings for dramatic effect. They did not lower their guns, but the family crossed themselves and there were whispers of El Diablo.

Chuck raised his hands to calm the small crowd. "Relax, he's only renting a room down there. He wishes he had that kind of power."

Bash moved to Laura's side and Watson positioned himself in front of them, teeth bared and ready.

Thomas rolled his eyes. "How rebellious and on

brand of you, Laura, to adopt a hellhound."

His once long, wavy hair was cut short and slicked back. Instead of the usual denim and leather, he wore black dress pants and a crisp white shirt. Across his neck was a grisly scar that marked where Adira had sunk her teeth during their last encounter.

His short haircut made his ice blue eyes more pronounced. They were the same eyes that looked out from Daniel and Sarah. While Daniel's were sharp and suspicious and Sarah's could be fierce, Thomas's eyes twinkled with amusement, even when he was trying to kill them. *Especially when he was trying to kill them.*

What she knew about genetics wouldn't fill a shot glass, but Laura wondered how her own eyes had ended up so green. Did it mean that she was more human than angel? She held her fireball in one hand and flicked at the short hair on his neck with the other. "You've adopted some new things, too."

"Aww, I knew you'd be the one to notice my haircut and you'll always be my favorite." He gave Sarah a disapproving look. "Anyway, I thought it might make me look more like your Uncle Daniel." He put his mouth close to her ear. "Speaking of whom, beware of angels in sheep's clothing, my dear."

She pulled the fire into a thick band between her hands. "I'm tired, Thomas. What do you want?"

"I brought a gift for the birthday girl." He winked at Tina. "But I also have a gift for you."

He held up the frame and, since she wouldn't let go of her fire band, Bash took it from him. The woman in the picture was the spitting image of Laura. She was younger than Laura when the photo was taken, but they shared the same coppery hair and emerald eyes. It was obvious from her clothes and hairstyle that the picture was from some time in the forties. The two women could have been twins out of time, but Laura's features were softer, and her expressions were usually warm and thoughtful. The woman in the photo had sharp facial lines and a stony, calculating stare.

"Who is this?"

"Be quiet, Sebastian, this is a family matter." Thomas put a finger to his lips and turned to Laura, announcing, "I've been doing some genealogy and I thought it might be of interest to you."

Sarah took the frame from Bash and looked from Laura to the picture and back. "This must be Fiona." Thomas had mentioned their grandmother once before, and even he seemed to dislike her.

Sarah shrugged and said, "We've never met this woman."

Thomas cupped his hands over his mouth and whispered, "She's still alive."

They were interrupted by a bright flash and a soft fluttering sound. Tina had pulled the ribbon from the gift Thomas gave her and as the four sides of the box fell open, a whirlwind of glittering confetti sized gems encircled the girl.

She was not its prey though and Tromluí was a bit weak from imprisonment. It swirled through the crowd darting between family and friends before brushing against Bash, who was definitely one of its targets. It tried to surround him but Sarah extended her arms and used her power to push it over the fence.

"Knock it off." Laura snapped at Thomas and looked away from him and the picture. "I don't care who that is, I don't want anything to do with her or you."

As Laura manipulated the fire in her hands, Mena could sense her friend's waning patience and pointed at the gate. "Get off of my property."

Thomas shifted his eyes from Mena to Chuck and said to her, "I like that you're the one in charge of this house. Do you know that strong women like you will shape the future of this world?"

Bash took a step forward. "You heard her."

Thomas curled his lip. "Don't give me a reason, cowboy."

Chuck and Drew were at Bash's side in an instant and Watson began a low, menacing growl.

Thomas shrugged and returned his attention to Laura. Touching her face, he said. "You really should do something about those little lines around your eyes. It shouldn't be that hard. You are a witch, after all." As he touched her, Laura pulled on his power and the flame in her hands swelled until he had to move away.

He glared at Bash. "Or maybe you could just lose 200 pounds. That's done wonders for your sister's complexion."

At his mention of Rueben's death, Sarah lunged at Thomas. "You bastard!"

Drew grabbed her by the waist and held her back. Unmoved, Thomas flapped his wings at the crowd, then tucked them away as he left the yard followed by Watson who nudged the gate closed behind him.

Chapter Three

After a long hot shower, Laura dressed in one of Bash's t-shirts and a pair of his old boxer shorts. It turned him on when she wore his clothes and if he'd had an ounce of extra energy, he would have taken them right back off of her. Instead, as they crawled into his bed, he spooned her tightly against his chest while lying on his side to protect his back and they fell into a deep sleep.

She woke to his jerking body and frightened gasps a few hours later as a nightmare took hold of him. Taking his face in her hands, she whispered, "Shh…Sebastian, it's me."

His eyes snapped open and it took several seconds, but finally he recognized her. She smoothed his hair back and kissed his lips. "We're safe."

It enraged her to see him tortured like that and she would not have been surprised if the others were suffering the same sleepless nights. After all they'd been through, how could they not? Her friends deserved, at the very least, to get some decent sleep in between crises and she silently vowed to come up with a ward to protect them from their dreams.

He pushed the comforter away and rested his head on her belly, moaning with pleasure as she massaged his scalp with her fingertips. The terror of his dream forgotten, a fresh, urgent need awakened in him and he nibbled on her hip while tugging at the boxer shorts.

"Do you want me, baby?"

Skin tingling with yearning, she arched her body into him, and, encouraged, he left wet kisses across her middle.

She gripped his arms, "I want you, Bash."

He pulled the t-shirt over her head and rolled his tongue around her nipples, slipping his leg between hers, then kissing his way along her throat in search of her lips.

Lately when they made love, it was often rushed and the experience was becoming more like a reward for survival than an expression of their feelings for one another. Though they were still reeling from the day's events, he took his time that night, moving his hands along her curves with purpose and following up with his tongue.

Her fingers flowed across his body and he nuzzled her ear, growling low as she pleased him. His murmurs of "Yeah," and "Just like that", made her crazy with desire. Her enthusiasm for him fueled his passion and his kisses grew hungrier as he positioned her beneath him.

When at last he slid into her, groaning, "God damn, woman," She couldn't help but cry out for him, closing her eyes and savoring the slow, deep movement of his body inside of hers.

Mindful of his wounds, she raked her fingernails

down his lower back and over his hips, pulling him even closer as her pleasure mounted. "Harder Bash, you feel so good."

His body tightened and as his thrusts became more powerful, she ran her tongue along his neck, took his earlobe between her teeth, and whispered, "I'm coming for you."

She wrapped her legs around him and he lost control, murmuring her name over and over as their bodies shuddered against one other.

He collapsed into her arms, panting, "Wow, that was good." They rested like that for a while before he rolled onto his back, forgetting about his injury. "Ow, shit." He jerked upright when the sheets scraped against his back, but he grinned and propped a pillow under his chin.

She narrowed her eyes at him. "You seem pleased with yourself."

He laughed out loud. "You bet I'm pleased with myself—an old man like me, making you scream like that?"

Her smile faded. "You're only a year older than I am."

"Hey." He traced his finger along her collar bone. "Remember that you weren't the only one making noise in this bed tonight, baby. You drive me wild."

They drifted back to sleep, relishing the relaxed, happy feeling that washed over them, temporarily forcing the recent battle from their minds.

"Hey buddy," Chuck said.

Bash croaked out something along the lines of

"Hello," and moved the phone from his ear to squint at the clock, which read 5:10 am.

"We've got an early one—I'll pick you up in thirty minutes."

While he rushed to get ready for work, Laura made coffee and fixed him a quick breakfast sandwich.

She noticed when she fed Watson that next to the food was a new basket which contained a few balls and a leash. Bash had already purchased a special bowl for her dog and kept plenty of treats in his pantry for when they stayed with him.

Watson slept at the foot of Laura's bed when they were home alone, but when visiting Bash, there wasn't enough room for the three of them in his bed so Bash had searched online until he found a dog bed large enough. For a brief moment, she let herself imagine him and Watson taking long walks and playing ball together if she moved in.

She held up a pair of his sweatpants. "Can I borrow these to go home in?" Her ruined clothes had gone in the trash before her shower the night before.

He put down his sandwich and stopped her from gathering up her other things. "Wait, wait, wait. You don't have to leave."

She blinked at him. "I…I guess I don't have to go right this minute."

He lifted her chin to meet her eyes with his. "Did you think about what I asked you last night?"

She gave him a coy smile. "You know I did."

"That sounds hopeful."

"We need to talk about things like finances and—"

"What?" He cut her off. "Don't worry about that stuff."

She blinked at him again.

He slid his holster onto his belt and clipped his badge next to it just as Chuck's horn blared from the driveway. Downing the last of his coffee, he took her into his arms. "Baby, just pick a moving date and I'll take care of everything else."

She tapped her fingers on the grip of his revolver. "Be careful today."

Bits of memory from the night before—how she looked when they fought the harpies and the feel of her tongue on his skin—flashed through his mind as he kissed her. "I have an awful lot to live for." He put on his hat and gave her a wink as he walked out the door.

She and Watson stood still in the silence for a little while, then the dog followed her as she wandered in circles through the house. She made up the bed in Bash's room and opened the closet. His clothes hung on one side and a large gun safe was mounted to the back wall. The rest of the space was empty but for his winter coat and boots. She smiled at this because everyone in the valley had a heavy coat and boots but usually only dusted them off when traveling up north.

Next to his coat hung the satin nightgown she'd bought especially for his birthday back in July. He had a thing for zippers and was thrilled to learn that the bodice of the gown unzipped all the way to her navel.

He used the second bedroom as an office, which contained a wooden desk, his chair, and a short file cabinet, upon which sat an ancient ink jet printer. He worked out in that room as well, so various weights lined the wall opposite the desk. A sweat towel he'd forgotten to pick up after his last workout rested in a lump on the floor next to a foam roller.

On one side of his laptop sat the Millennium Falcon desk lamp she bought him for Christmas. They were seven and eight years old when Star Wars first premiered and one of their favorite dates was spent under a blanket on his couch rewatching Episodes Four, Five, and Six back-to-back.

On the other side was the selfie she'd taken of them in Sedona. She hadn't realized that he'd printed it out and her heart swelled a bit when she held it up. The simple wooden frame he selected showed off the beauty of the red rocks in the background, but their laughter was the star of the shot. They took that trip before she found out her father was a fallen angel and before they were drafted into heaven's war.

She plucked the dirty towel off the floor and walked it to the laundry room down the hall. She considered her house to be well kept, but if that was his idea of a mess, she could reasonably be called the slob of the operation.

A large oval-shaped rug with red and black geometric patterns covered much of the tile floor, but otherwise the third bedroom was empty. She opened the closet to find three bankers boxes lined up across the top shelf. The boxes were labeled ARMY, BECKY, and KEEP.

She could guess what was in the ARMY box and assumed the BECKY box held records from the legal battles with his ex-mother-in-law for custody of his daughter after his wife died. When Becky went to college and Bash was finally able to contact her without his mother-in-law hovering, he and his daughter were slowly able to build up a schedule of monthly calls.

Becky appreciated her grandmother's intentions but

resented being kept from her father for all those years, and Bash was cautiously optimistic that they could make something of a relationship as she grew into adulthood. There were things he'd bought for her and saved for her in that box and Laura figured he intended to simply hand over the whole thing one day.

She would have to speculate on the KEEP box. Photo albums? High School yearbooks? Han Solo action figure? His mother had been cremated…good god, was she in there? In any case, the room would make the perfect guest space as well as an office for Bountiful Botanicals, minus that ugly rug.

She ended her tour back at the kitchen table and finished up her coffee that had gone cold. It was obvious that she could fit into his house and she was overcome with a fresh wave of emotion as she finally realized it. She loved him so much, but she'd never lived with a man. Sarah would say she was being dramatic, but at her age, the notion of trusting him with every piece of her life every single day was terrifying.

She stood abruptly, cleared their dishes, grabbed her things, and locked the front door behind her. Outside, Watson tilted his head with concern as she doubled over against her Jeep and took several deep breaths. She wasn't sure if she was feeling anxiety or elation but either way, she'd just decided to move in with Sebastian Scott.

* * *

"Did you say attempted rape?" Bash was skeptical as they pulled into the emergency room parking lot. "Around here?"

Cases of domestic violence plagued the Sheriff's department, but most people tried to lay low in their town and Chuparosa was relatively free of other types of violent crime.

Though Chuck didn't respond, his expression was grim, and Bash knew what he was thinking. His daughter, Tina, and Audi and Missy were supposed to get together after Tina's party. The young women still lived at home and frequently met around a fire pit in the desert with a bottle of wine. It was a cheap way for them to hang out away from their parents.

The others demurred when Missy's boyfriend invited himself along, so it was just her and Josh by the fire when Missy was attacked. Chuck's concern extended beyond his own house, though. Only a few months earlier, Sarah's daughter, Audi, had been kidnapped. That crime was, he hoped, unrelated, but the targeting of Chuparosa's women, for any reason, was becoming a worrying trend.

Missy Trainor's parents were talking to the doctor and a forensic nurse when the deputies arrived. David Trainor was a social worker for the state in an office downtown and his wife, Sonia, stayed at home with their surprise, late in life seven-year-old twin boys.

Sonia was also a member of a local coven calling themselves the Desert Doves. Laura was friendly with them, but they'd never invited her to join. It was understood that Laura didn't participate in organized religion of any kind, and she made them nervous anyway. They did, however, extend each other professional *courtesies* from time to time.

Sonia paced around the nurse, who was packing away her camera in a soft-sided duffel bag, while David addressed the deputies. His voice was measured in the clinical way that social workers speak when trying to detach themselves from a situation. "It appears he was unsuccessful with a sexual assault, Sheriff. We'll be taking her home in a little while."

Sonia, on the other hand, was not detached at all. "Sheriff, you should know that I intend to hex that man."

Chuck winced. "Why don't you let us find him first, Sonia?"

Audi and Tina pushed through the doors and made a beeline to the gurney where Missy sat shivering and picking at her fingernails. Audi glared at the insensitive doctor and snatched a blanket from a warming cabinet. Once she was covered, Missy became quite animated and began to share her story with her friends.

Rather than make her repeat the whole thing later, Bash hurried over and interrupted, "Can you start at the beginning for me, Missy?"

"Yeah." The girl heaved an impatient sigh. "So, like I said, Josh and I were hanging out by the natural bridge. You know the one, with the rows of big rocks next to the riverbed?"

Bash nodded.

"Well, I had to pee, so I went behind that Creosote bush..."

Chuck approached with his phone at his ear and one finger held up, motioning for Bash to join him a few feet away. He ended the call and said, "I talked to Josh. Whoever did this knocked him clean out and he didn't see a thing."

"Where is he now?"

"In the cafeteria. The kid's pretty shaken up, so I

called Drew to sit with him for a while. He's finishing up a job at the Baptist church, but he'll be here soon. Remember when we busted those kids last week for messing with the breaker box?"

"Nice of the church to give Drew the work."

Chuck sniffed. "I suspect he offered to do it for free."

Drew's day job was that of a sought-after electrician who spent several days a month working in expensive homes across the valley. He spent the rest of his time building up his church's congregation and helping out around Chuparosa.

They turned their attention back to Missy, who was showing her friends a series of bruises on her forearm.

Bash held out his hand and said, "May I?"

She nodded, and he cast Chuck a glance while gingerly examining the darkening spots where the girl had been grabbed.

Chuck's jaw tightened. "What time did you get out there?"

"I didn't check—maybe one o'clock or so. Josh didn't get even off work until eleven. Are you guys done? Can I finish my story, please?"

Bash suppressed a smile and stared down at his notebook "Yes ma'am, go ahead."

She twisted the folds of the blanket between her fingers and continued, "When I was done at the bush, he grabbed me from behind. Like I said before," she glared at her parents, "he wasn't trying to have sex with me because he waited for me to pull up my pants. He said I couldn't 'cross over' with him until I answered his question."

Chuck's brow furrowed. "Cross over with him?"

She shrugged and pushed her hair behind her ears. "It was ultra-weird."

"Do you remember the question?"

"It was just a creepy poem about something large and small, curved and straight." She shrugged and raised her palms. "Sheriff, he's just crazy. He got real mad when I couldn't answer."

Chuck's phone rang and when he stepped away, Bash pressed her, "Do you think you could describe him?"

"I *said* he grabbed me from behind." She looked down at her lap, adding, "It was dark, and he whispered everything in my ear."

"How'd you get away?"

Tina folded her arms across her chest and said, "We watch all the true crime shows now, since Audi got taken, I mean."

Missy bobbed her head in agreement. "I kicked out his shin and reached behind me to scratch his face. We know that they'll take samples from underneath your nails and they might be able to catch him even if he kills you."

Bash raised his eyebrows, "You left a mark on his face?"

"That's not my blood." She proudly let him inspect the grimy fingernails on her other hand.

Rage percolated in Bash's chest as he wondered if his own twenty-something daughter was streaming true crime for tips on how to exist in the world. He patted her shoulder and said, "You did good, Missy."

Chuck put his phone in his pocket and motioned for Bash to join him at the back of the room.

"They finally got a new ranger working the park.

Some guy from Tucson named..." he checked his notes. "...Richard Jeffries. Let's go talk to him."

Bash made a face. "Ranger Rick? Are you fucking kidding me?"

Chuck snorted. "At the very least, he can help us search the area, man."

Bash ran a hand through his hair. "The natural bridge is behind Laura's house."

Chapter Four

Temecula Street was shorter than the others on the Chuparosa grid since the houses were built as close as they could be to Shock Butte. Shock Butte was so called because of the handful of residents over the years who had been struck by lightning at the top. Of note is that while those individuals could not be charged with specific crimes, Chuparosa had a way of weeding out folks who were not a good...fit.

Laura lived on the west side of the street, three houses down from the butte. Like Sarah, she did not have a traditional backyard. It was more of an expansive cactus garden that she never bothered to fence in. Closer to the house was her immense container herb garden and an avocado tree that she and Brian grew from a seed when he was seven years old.

Though they made for a scorching summertime, she had several west facing windows and nothing blocked her view of the sun setting over the peaks. She bought the quaint two-bedroom house just after Brian was born and it was on a morning walk with her new baby that she discovered the natural bridge.

There were no official trails in that area so she took him straight out the back door for two miles, following the curve at the base of the butte until she came across what was once a colossal pale rock that had been obliterated over time into piles of somewhat smaller rocks leading to a dry riverbed.

Rhonda told her once that the river used to run during monsoon season with rainwater flowing down from the mountains, but Laura rarely saw water running in any of the rivers in the valley and never once in Chuparosa.

Canyon walls rose farther down the riverbed, jutting with stone ledges and pocked with caves. She guessed that the county deemed the spot far too dangerous to include in the public park and chose to ignore it. She had always been fascinated by the area though and, as far as she knew, only her family and a handful of others were aware of its existence.

Two days after Missy's attack, Audi brought Laura, Watson, and Sarah to the bridge and the exact site of her friends' fireside chats.

"We never cross the bridge," she was quick to explain. "Missy and Josh were on a blanket over there." She stepped across a piece of Saguaro skeleton and led them to a clearing roughly fifty yards away where the girls had arranged a circle of rocks for their fires.

"How did he even get out here?" Laura wondered. "There's no road, and no trail."

"I think it's time for you to build that fence around your house." Sarah cautioned.

Laura dug in her pack for one of Watson's favorite peanut butter treats. "That will be the future owner's problem."

Audi did not even try to hide her disappointment. "So, you're really going to do it, Auntie?"

"Laura put her hands on her hips. "You don't approve?"

"Don't get me wrong," she twisted her hair in her fingers, "I like the Sheriff a lot, it's just the wagon load of red flags he pulls behind him that makes me nervous. He already hurt you once."

"Audra, please," Sarah scoffed, "Our wagons aren't exactly empty, not even yours."

"Hey, what's that over there?" The others shaded their eyes with their hands and followed Laura's pointed finger to a light flickering in the canyon past the bridge. "Is it coming from a cave?"

Followed by Watson, she headed off in that direction until Sarah stopped her. "It's another couple of miles away and that creep could be hiding there."

Laura scratched at the phosphorescent polish on her fingernails until a flame jumped into her hand. "Have you got something better to do right now?"

"Ew," Laura and Sarah looked back and laughed as Audi swatted away thin white spider webs that had been spun throughout the bushes they passed. While distracted, Laura felt her foot catch on something and the next thing she knew, her knees, and then her hands hit the ground. She didn't get her arms locked out in time to keep her chin from skidding across the sand and she fell flat on her face.

Watson whined, nudging his nose into her hair, and Audi shrieked, "Auntie!"

Dazed, Laura rolled onto her back and touched the bloody patch on her chin. "Good god, what just happened to me?"

"You tripped over this." Sarah kicked the Saguaro skeleton out of the way and knelt beside her.

"Wait a minute," Audi picked it up, "that thing was *way* over there before."

"Crap, Lolly," Sarah winced, "Look at your knees."

"That was a nasty fall." The man walking toward them across the bridge had no sooner uttered the words when he heard three simultaneous clicks and found himself staring down the barrels of three .38 specials.

He put his hands up. "Hey, now."

Sarah glared at him. "Who are you? Where did you come from?"

"I've become partial to the name Richard Jeffries, ma'am, and I'm sure not here to hurt you."

"Speaking of red flags..." Sarah whispered to her sister.

He was shorter than them by several inches and appeared to be much younger. He had long, wavy gray hair pulled back into a ponytail at the nape of his neck and secured with a wide, elaborately embroidered elastic. His muscles bulged underneath the short sleeves of his shirt and there were three zig zag marks running down the side of his face, near his ear.

Laura thought it must have been a birth mark that he was ashamed of because he'd made sure the ponytail was loose enough for his hair to partially cover it. He had matching tattoos around his forearms of symbols that made no sense to her.

She sat up on her elbow, still aiming at his forehead, and recognized the County Parks and Recreation logo on his olive-green uniform shirt along with the patch confirming his name.

"You must be the new ranger." She lowered her pistol and tried to stand, but Sarah held her back.

"Hang on, you've got a hundred little rocks buried in your skin." She holstered her pistol and poked around in her backpack for her first aid kit.

Richard stepped around Sarah. "You see, the most dangerous parts of the trails are the flats." He took a knee beside Laura and zipped off the leg of her torn hiking pants. "You're actually safer when you're climbing around because that's when you're paying more attention."

Audi, who had not holstered her gun, huffed in disgust and said to her mother, "He's not trying to mansplain hiking is he?"

He carried himself like a man who was perpetually overcompensating for an insecurity that had been leveled on him at some point by a bully. It appeared to them that over time, Richard had become the bully himself, or was at least trying to.

He slid the detached leg of her pants down to her boot and ran his hand up her calf. "Let me help you out." He plucked a piece of gravel from the skin on her knee. "See, these are basic sandstone but," he held it up to the sun, "still beautiful, just like you."

Laura shuddered and twisted away from him. She was already shaken by the fall and he was making her very uncomfortable.

"She's fine." Sarah stepped around him and extended her hand to Laura, assuring him, "it looks worse than it is."

Richard hovered near them as they helped Laura hobble to a seat on a large sun-bleached rock.

"That there's limestone. Say, do you like riddles?"

"She's not in kindergarten," Sarah snapped. "You don't need to distract her from the pain."

Undeterred, he leaned over and spoke to Laura in a sing song voice, "There is something I can see, tell me, tell me, what can it be?"

"Go away, Dr. Seuss." Audi cocked her pistol near his head.

He seemed unconcerned, and continued, "It could be large or small or curved or straight. Sometimes it's deadly and sometimes it's harmless, but it was here before you, so it remains blameless. Tell me now, on the double, what is this thing that gives desert men so much trouble?"

Laura did not go to college and in dark moments thought herself stupid around her family and friends who did. However, there were two skills in which she outshined them all. She was an excellent trivia game partner, and she could solve riddles. Brian had been a serious little boy and she spent many hours solving riddles with him when he was young. In fact, just the day before, he had texted her from school with a good one.

Richard, in her opinion, had not come up with a good one. "A desert creature...sometimes deadly, sometimes harmless?" She smirked at him. "Do you use that one on your kid tours?"

His eyes hardened. "Do you know the answer or not?"

She lifted her chin, "It's a scorpion's tail."

The corners of his mouth curled into a smile and he held out his hand. "Now you can come across with me, and we'll have a real talk."

Audi snorted, "Dude, seriously?"

Sarah stepped between him and her sister. "There's nothing over the bridge."

Just then dust began to swirl beneath Laura's feet and as she stood to move away, Tromluí pushed itself upward in a gust of wind, nearly knocking her down again as it's funnel of tiny crystals travelled over her and Watson.

"Pfthe," she sputtered and waved her hands in front of her.

Richard took her by the arm and Watson began to bark. The ranger backed away, but he seemed no more anxious about the dog than he was about Audi's gun. "I'm just trying to make friends."

"Well," Sarah said brusquely, "thanks but we've got this handled."

They took advantage of the distractions and limped away with Laura, leaving Richard literally in the dust. He folded his arms and called after them, "That's okay, you'll be back soon, and then we'll talk."

Then he spat into the wind carrying Tromluí away, "Have your fun, spirit, but the angel witch is mine."

* * *

"I'm just saying that being part angel should come with better benefits," Audi complained as she, Laura, Bash, and Drew pushed through the front doors of the YMCA. "Like perpetually smooth skin or something. We don't even get wings and that's bullshit."

"Middle school didn't suck bad enough for you?" Laura asked patiently.

Since Audi's kidnapping a few months earlier, she hadn't been able to sleep, and her attitude was all over the place. At Sarah's request, Bash arranged to get her into the Y's martial arts class led by a Sifu who lived in town. Their hope was that she would soon feel more in control and regain the confidence she'd lost that night.

They had also come together that evening to help Laura. Her doctor suggested adding weight training to her hiking and yoga regimens to stave off osteoporosis in the years to come. Audi's point about angel anatomy was not lost on Laura, who herself did not believe she should have to contend with the indignities of aging. Too proud to ask Daniel about it, and excited by the prospect of getting stronger, she had decided to hire the female fitness coach who advertised in the tri-cities newspaper.

When they heard about her plans, Bash and Drew insisted that they could teach her instead. She wasn't particularly interested in listening to them go on about all the heavy things but thought it might be fun to work out with her boyfriend on occasion.

For his part, Bash was looking to shake things up a bit. Over the years he'd added several sets with barbells, but otherwise had woken with the sun for decades to complete the same workout the Army taught him as a teenager.

After turning fifty, he bought himself a fitness tracker and the first thing he learned was that he was not as fast or as strong as he thought he was. *As he used to be.* It wasn't surprising information, but it was unpleasant to see the daily statistics flash across his wrist. He feared that rather than tracking progress, the device was just a means to document his slow decline. So, he returned it and decided instead to try a few new things, being more likely to see improvement at something as a beginner.

He was a decent swimmer and thought that if Brian didn't hate him so much, Laura's son could teach him a good swimming set—something easier on his joints than all that running. Water sports aside, he also wanted to make things right with that young man as soon as he could.

Drew liked being around people and often worked out at the YMCA so, unlike the others, he was quite comfortable there. He cast a glance back at the door. "Is Sarah coming tonight?"

Laura frowned. "I guess not." She invited her sister but had only received a half-hearted "we'll see" in response.

Audi sniffed. "She's barely talked to me since we met Richard the Riddler."

"The new park ranger?" Drew asked.

Laura scowled. "The way he touched my legs made my skin crawl."

Bash clenched his jaw. "He touched you?"

"I had a pistol in my hand so he wasn't going to get away with anything else."

Drew shot Bash a look and said, "Still, that was pretty ballsy."

Laura shook off the memory, announcing, "I don't like him, and I don't want to talk about him."

She stepped between the men and squeezed their biceps. "I guess it's gonna be Sarah's loss tonight."

Her gaze then zeroed in on a young man walking toward them in a tank top with the word "Instructor" printed across the chest. "Look Audi, muscles everywhere."

Bash sighed, "This was a terrible idea. While I get

Audi settled, can you please do something about that?"

The instructor was asking Laura about her fitness goals and leading her to the weight racks, so Drew laughed and dutifully put himself in between the two of them.

As Bash left Audi's classroom, he caught sight of himself in the mirrored wall and ran a hand over his face. In that light, his beard was almost completely gray.

"Fuck that," he muttered and left to find the others.

Chapter Five

He told himself that he was just going to check on her, but when Drew stopped by Sarah's house on his way home from the gym, the truth was that he missed her. She hadn't been to his church meetings in weeks and he hadn't seen her since Tina's party.

She opened the door and set her wine glass on the entryway table, swaying a bit as she backed up to let him in. She was barefoot, wearing black leggings and a Depeche Mode t-shirt that he was pretty sure hadn't seen the light of day in at least thirty years.

His suspicion was confirmed by several dusty boxes in various stages of discovery throughout her living room. There was an empty wine bottle on the coffee table next to an open yearbook and a song by Kansas blared from the television as her favorite show began a new episode.

She grabbed the remote and turned it off. "Don't mind the mess, I was packing some things." She pulled at the bottom of her t-shirt and grinned at him. "Look what I found."

She scrunched up her nose at the sight of his sweaty workout clothes and tousled hair. "Oh crap, was that tonight? How did it go?"

Though he'd wanted to see her at the gym, he would rather have taken her out to dinner. He guessed that she'd lost at least ten pounds since Rueben's funeral.

"Yeah, it was tonight. By the way, Laura told us you ran into the new park ranger." A theory was forming in his mind and he hoped Sarah might fill in some of the details her sister hadn't wanted to discuss.

"Ugh, he was such a creep." She plucked a few crystals from an antique bowl on the coffee table and held them up one by one for affect. "This is limestone, and this is sandstone..." She dropped the crystals back into the dish. "He was obsessed with rocks – and Laura. You know, I believe Sebastian would have killed him if he had been there."

Drew nodded gravely, stepping around the boxes to pick the yearbook off the table. "Were you packing…or unpacking?"

She shrugged, turning in a circle amidst the mess. "Both, I guess. I have to leave this house or I will go insane."

He dropped the book and caught her as she stumbled. "Sarah, let me help you."

She leaned into his arms and rested her head on his chest. On the few occasions she dared to contemplate a fresh start, Sarah always convinced herself that a life with Andrew was one that she didn't deserve. If she'd had the courage to leave Rueben years ago when she knew their marriage was over, he would probably still be alive. She could hear her mother's voice in her head saying over and over, "You did this. You are an abomination."

The concern in Drew's eyes as she fell apart only made it worse. *If he really wants to help,* she thought to herself, *boy do I have an assignment for him.*

"I know exactly what you can do." She slid her hands under his t-shirt and caressed the skin just above his waistband. She knew it was the wine talking but maybe they could just have the experience and worry about the rest of it later. If he would throw her on the bed and fuck her senseless, then maybe for just a little while she wouldn't have to think about anything else.

Instead, he flinched away and held her at arm's length. "Sarah, stop." He took a ragged breath and tried to focus his racing mind. There were so many times he had dreamed of her touch but, no matter how he burned for her, he was not going to let it happen in that way.

She took his hands in hers and stepped close to him again, "Don't you think it's time?" She kissed him, but without responding, he pressed his hands gently against her shoulders and backed away once more. He knew he would lose control if he kissed her back and there would be no salvaging the relationship after that.

She was furious. "After everything that's happened, don't you dare turn me away now!"

"Turn you away?" He couldn't believe she'd said that to him. "All I want is to be close to you." He let his hands fall to his sides in frustration. "Sure, we could share our bodies with each other right now, but you *know* I want more. You *know* I love you and I won't complicate things when you are clearly in so much pain."

"Love me?" She sniffed. "You're too busy trying to

be the good guy."

His face fell. "You're right, and I shouldn't have come here tonight."

As he started for the door, she threw her arms in the air and sent him flying backward into the wall with her power. His body hovered for a moment in the crushed plaster behind him before sliding to the tile in a heap.

Horrified by what she'd done, she pressed her hands to her mouth and rushed to him. "Oh, my god, Andrew."

He put his hands up to stop her. "Don't touch me." He groaned and rose to his knees, grabbing the wall to pull himself up. She reached for him again, but he shouted, "I said don't touch me!"

He pushed off the wall and pulled open the front door, slamming it so hard on his way out that her wine glass toppled over and shattered to the floor.

Later at Isaac's Oasis, Chuck and Bash sat open-mouthed across from Drew as he relayed the story for them.

Chuck took a bite of his burger and mumbled, "You did the right thing, man."

Drew picked up a French fry. "I wish I'd come up with a more graceful exit." He put down the fry and stared at his plate. "I hate that I yelled at her."

Chuck shook his head. "She hurt your feelings, your pride, and your body—do you know how sore you're gonna be tomorrow?"

Drew picked up his French fry again, grimaced and let it fall back on the plate. "Thank god for cheap drywall or she might have broken my back."

Bash sipped his beer thoughtfully and said, "You know, I was married for thirteen years. At the end, Sherry hated me, my job, the Army," he chuckled, "and even my mom. No one went to counseling back then and I didn't know how to fix it." He took another sip. "Hell, I didn't want to fix it. We were only thirty-two but we were so unhappy. When she was killed," he rubbed his hand over his beard, preparing himself to say the next words. "No matter how much I wanted to, I...I didn't miss her and I hated myself for that."

"What Sarah did was wrong, but I understand what she's going through. Rueben made her miserable, and she was falling for you, so she feels guilty now that he's gone. It's tearing her apart and all you can do is wait to see if she gets her shit together." He met Drew's eyes. "You've been waiting for her a long time and no one's gonna blame you if you decide to move on."

To that point Chuck nodded at a table of two women across the room. "She's a little young, but Stacy is single. Her husband took off a couple years ago."

"She has a kid, too." Bash added, knowing how badly Drew longed to be a father.

"A *little* young? What is she, all of thirty-five?" Drew finally took a bite of one of his French fries and laughed. "Besides, the bar is at an all-time high now. If she can't throw me through a wall using her brain, then I don't want her."

Isaac brought them another round as Adam Colter took the seat next to Drew.

"Sorry I'm late, I had to check in at the office."

Adam was the night shift engineering supervisor at the utility company that shared an office with the

Sheriff's department. He'd offered his assistance with a bit of unconventional paperwork for the county after Thomas tried to blow up Chuck and Bash a few months earlier. Later, he helped Bash and Drew rewire some lights at the YMCA. They liked him well enough but didn't know much about him other than that he had *certain abilities*. Laura's good friend, Cara, had just moved in with Adam so Drew suggested they start inviting him out.

"What did I miss?"

They weren't going to rehash Drew's tragic love story for the new guy, so Chuck said, "We believe the new park ranger is a problem, so the preacher's been doing some research."

Drew looked around the table and hesitated. "You're gonna think I'm crazy."

Bash laughed, "Compared to what?"

"Well, we may be dealing with a bridge troll." He sat back in his chair as they stared at him. "I told you."

Isaac returned with Adam's order and a beer for himself and leaned against the table to get in on the conversation. "Harpy attacks and now trolls? Since when is the Other Side so interested us?

"Laura said this guy wore a county uniform." Bash turned to Chuck. "Didn't we get his file from Human Resources?"

Drew pulled a book from the satchel hanging on the back of his chair. "I'm not sure why he's impersonating a park ranger but look," he pushed his plate back and flipped through the pages, "it all checks out: the riddle, the obsession with rocks—I mean, he's even guarding the damn bridge. As far as we know, he hasn't made an appearance in any other location."

Adam shook his head. "I've seen some weird shit around here, but I don't believe I ever came across a troll. What do you suppose he wants?"

"I'm still trying to put that together, but you can bet he's going to make things worse for us."

"Naturally." Bash poked at the book. "Did you get all of this out of your Dictionary of Demons?"

Drew lifted the spine to show them. "The Encyclopedia of Spirits, actually."

"Jesus, you're killing me."

Isaac tipped his beer toward the door, "Speaking of..."

They turned in their chairs to see Daniel striding toward them. Remembering their last conversation with Adam, Bash grumbled, "Brace yourself—you said you wanted to meet an angel."

Adam shifted uncomfortably in his seat. "I did not say that. I asked if *you* had ever met an angel."

"Well, get ready to be disappointed."

"Where have you been?" Drew growled at Daniel under his breath.

Bash leaned forward and pushed his pointer finger into the table, "We're out here fighting harpies and shit with no sign from Heaven at all."

Daniel picked up Bash's beer bottle and gave it a sniff. "You are the sign, Sebastian."

"Hey!" He snatched it away.

"Isaac, may I have a bottle of that, and...?" He then pointed to a cheeseburger on the menu card and said, "Thank you."

"I'm guessing you can't pay for this," Isaac said as he left for the kitchen, "so, thank them."

Bash cocked his head in disbelief, but Daniel

shrugged his shoulders and turned his attention to the newest man in the group.

"Hello, Adam." The angel eyed him, but not with the contempt Adam had expected. "Will you be joining us regularly?"

Adam found Daniel's demeanor comforting and disturbing at the same time. He was cool and reserved as if he had little to no concern how Adam answered his question but that, somehow, he could still get it wrong.

"I suppose that's up to these guys, but would it be a problem for you if I did?"

The others leaned in, fascinated by the exchange as they'd never seen Daniel quite so on his guard. If you weren't paying close attention, he looked like every other man in the place wearing boots, jeans, and a button-down shirt. Adam studied him carefully though, and either they couldn't see it or Bash and his friends were used to the subtle ways in which Daniel stood out in a crowd. There were strands of pure silver streaking through his dark hair and the light reflected off his skin in such a way that made other people avert their gaze without realizing it.

Adam knew for sure the other men couldn't see the spirits that hovered around Daniel. The bar was old and home to many souls desperate for answers and who would be able to recognize an angel a mile away. They danced around him the way children do when they have something to show you and Daniel treated them with the indifference of an exhausted parent.

"Are you going to ignore them all night?" Adam asked, reaching out to gently brush away the arm of a spirit draped across Bash's shoulders. "He's taken, sweetheart."

Bash's spine prickled and he looked sideways at Drew, who began a mental list of questions to ask Adam at a more appropriate time.

Daniel's face softened a bit and he said, "If it will make you happy, I will speak with all of them before I leave."

"You didn't answer my first question." Adam had no delusions about his salvation, but he wondered how much of his story Daniel would feel compelled to share with the others. It wasn't the best kept secret in the world, but he wanted to let his new friends know in his own time.

"I'm sure you and I can work something out," Daniel offered, "I'm not here to make your life any harder than it has to be."

"No, just *our* lives." Chuck complained.

"Where would I get dinner money?"

Chuck rubbed his temples. "I meant that Bash was hurt, man."

"Oh. Yes, I know. And he used his torn flesh to lure the beasts to their destruction." Daniel looked Bash up and down. "Well done. That's why you and your friends are part of Heaven's watch over earth."

"Heaven's watch?"

"Humans were given this place in the universe because they were favored above all others and, remarkably, they still hold that favor. So, *you* are the sign, the sign to those who would try to take your home that Heaven's Defenses—her Watch—will not allow it."

"If I'm going to be one of these Defenses," Chuck started. "I'd like to lobby for a better insurance plan."

"Your point is well taken Chuck, but none of this is up to you."

"You should let Thomas know," Chuck said, "he thinks we all have free will."

"It's not about will, it's about destiny. Yes, everyone has free will, but some people have the option to play a bigger role if they choose." Daniel focused on Chuck as he continued, "Did you ever think of leaving all of this to them?" He gestured around the table. "These men wouldn't question it if you took your family to a safer place."

"No, man." Chuck blanched at the notion. "Why would you ask me that? These are my friends and Chuparosa is my town."

Daniel took one of Drew's abandoned French fries. "You were escaping your past, Andrew, and your vehicle broke down right outside of town. You didn't have to stay here but it sure felt right, didn't it?"

He peered at Bash's leftovers. "Sebastian, is it fair to say that your personal struggles guided you to Chuparosa as well?" Bash covered his plate and said nothing.

"I don't know why myself, but some people are supposed to be in certain places and they are lost until they get there. Chuck, you were simply here first."

"That don't make me feel special."

"Well," Bash snarked, "a map would have been nice."

Daniel shook his head. "I doubt you would have seen the bigger picture even if Laura's love was promised to you at the time. That the Deane sisters became our allies, more or less, confuses me still." He downed his beer in one long gulp. "But I don't ask questions, I just do my job."

"What happens to the people who don't find their

place?" Still convinced that salvation would forever elude him, Adam was suddenly very interested in his destiny.

"They die. But not like everyone else. They die knowing that something was left undone."

"I'm sure you didn't come here just to give us this pep talk," Drew said dryly.

"Of course not." Daniel's tone perked up, "As the veil thins, sacred places like your Chuparosa will no longer be the only ports of entry to and from the Other Side. Something is attempting to take advantage of that and merge a portal here with an opening near a denser population. It hasn't happened in this country yet but imagine, if you will, harpies flying over Phoenix."

Drew shuddered. "Thomas crashed Tina's party, so we know he fixed his gate."

Bash sat back and thought for a moment. "Nah, that's his private elevator in and out of Hell. Besides, he wants Chuparosa all to himself and he doesn't care about anything else."

Chuck put his beer bottle to his forehead. "I wonder if Missy Trainer stumbled onto something messing around near the bridge."

Bash nodded. "Maybe…let's talk to her again tomorrow. Then we'll see what this ranger troll is all about." He gritted his teeth. "He put his hands on Laura. If nothing else, I'm damn sure gonna talk to him about that."

Chapter Six

Tromluí lay stretched across the dirt along the driver's side of Bash's big black truck. As he approached, Tromluí blew a few rocks in the air, causing him to fumble his keys. He swore and knelt to pick them up, and as his knee touched the ground, the sand pushed itself into a circle around him.

"What the hell?" He tried to step out of the circle, but Tromluí swirled its crystal-like mass within the grains of sand and formed a miniature tornado that made its way up the length of his body and held him there.

Bash waved his arms, swatting at the dust surrounding him, then closed his eyes and held his breath as it spread across his chest and over his throat. It covered his entire body within seconds, suffocating him with a fine sheen of grit. When he thought he was sure to pass out from lack of air, it travelled over his head, tossing his cowboy hat across the dirt parking lot.

As the dust devil moved away, Bash fell against the truck and sucked in as many breaths as he could without hyperventilating. The circle around him dissolved and the sand spiral made a deep line in the dirt until it reached his hat, picked it up, and hurled it back to where he sat wheezing on the running board. Then the sand fell out of the spiral and what Bash thought for a moment was a fragmented ball of light disappeared into the darkness.

"Jesus Christ." He dusted himself off and got to his feet. "This night just keeps getting weirder." Dust devils were as common as dust itself in the desert, but even in Chuparosa they didn't usually try to kill a man. Grumbling, he slapped his hat against his thigh and put it on.

Nothing could ground him like holding Laura but, since she'd known he was going out, she'd made plans of her own. He hoped that soon they'd come home to each other every night, but she hadn't mentioned moving in since he cut her off about finances and he was uncomfortable with how his proposal was stagnating.

He could manage their few bills just fine and he probably should have explained that, but he'd been anxious since asking her in the first place. It was a clumsier, more aggressive delivery than he'd planned and she was caught off guard. Since they had so much to talk about, he considered tracking her down and wrestled with that idea for a while but, in the end, he settled on a text instead.

He hit send and his phone was ringing by the time he climbed into his truck.

"I'm going to be here at Rhonda's for a little while yet," she said, "how was your night?"

He gave her the quick highlights of Andrew's

suspicions, Adam's strange behavior, and Daniel's latest assignment, but left out her sister's breakdown and the murderous pile of dirt.

"Good god."

"Daniel is getting more serious about our role as Defenses."

"Daniel can kiss my ass, but I'll check with Adira because she may know something about this troll."

"Hey," he started, "is uh, Sarah with you?"

"No, why?"

"Just be careful out there, baby."

He smiled to himself when she whispered, "I love you," and hung up.

* * *

"Try it again." Rhonda prompted.

Laura exhaled and waved her hand around the burned patches that still smoldered in Rhonda's back yard.

"Are you sure? Your lemons...."

Well over half of the lemon tree branches drooped; charred and dripping from where they had doused the flames with the hose.

"Keep your focus and you won't lose control of it. You know what to do."

To spare what remained of the yard, they moved the experiment underneath the new protective carport that Bash, Drew, and Noah had built over a concrete slab in Rhonda's back yard. She could no longer get in and out of her beloved ancient pickup without pain, so she parked it out there and bought a small used car to get around town.

When Bash offered to sell the old truck for her, she said only if he would sell his old Stetson hat and the conversation was over.

Laura moved the truck out front and stood alone in the center of the slab. The carport had no walls so it would be easy enough to dive out of the way if something went wrong. She shoved her phone in her back pocket and rubbed her palms together.

"Remember…go slow." Rhonda coached. The older woman pulled at her sweaty blouse and wiped her brow. Though the wind had picked up, the air was getting heavier. Lightning flashed in the distance and if it was going to head west from Phoenix, a monsoon thunderstorm would be on top of them before they knew it. "But, not too slow."

Fire and electricity were not always available for her to harness, so Laura wanted to see if she could generate power from within herself, if only briefly, to defend them from an attack. They hadn't expected it to work so well and Rhonda's yard paid the price.

Watson moved closer in support and she relaxed her body, closing her eyes and moving her hands back and forth against each other until she felt the heat rise from between them. Then she crossed her arms and rubbed her hands on her shoulders. She could feel the static building between her and the flannel shirt of Bash's that she wore over her tank top.

As before, thin strands of blue light slipped in and out of her fingers. She moved her hands apart, and extended her arms at her sides, stretching the static into long ribbons.

Rhonda picked up a small rug and shook it, flinging dust particles which Laura reached out to with the static electricity. Sparks ignited midair, but that time she was able to latch onto them and rather than exploding a fireball over the yard with her power, she grew and then shrank the flames until they were only ashes fluttering to the ground.

Watson yipped his approval but except for the devious twinkle in her eyes, Laura's expression remained neutral. "If only I could have done *that* for the eighth-grade science fair."

She re-parked the truck out back and found Rhonda in the kitchen pouring them each a glass of iced tea. "Let's not teach Sarah that trick, just yet." Rhonda warned.

Though both sisters could work spells better than any witch she'd ever known, the more she thought about it, Rhonda doubted they could teach Sarah that skill at all. Laura could move fire and Sarah could move air and for years Rhonda had helped them try to copy each other's powers, but it seemed as though they were limited in the elements they could control. Since even their children inherited their specific skills, the abilities didn't appear to cross over generations either. *Just as well.*

Laura was drenched with sweat and gratefully accepted the tea as she peeled off the flannel shirt.

"Sarah's spells are getting better and better, and it's good that she's working on something," she thought for a moment and added, "this will sound awful, but I didn't expect her to be grieving so hard."

Rhonda gave Watson a treat and, ever protective, he followed them to the living room and stretched out between the ladies and the front door.

"I know he never moved out, but her husband

abandoned her years ago. It's more than grief, Laura. It's guilt and its fear, and that's a dangerous combination to be weaving through her magic. Especially with Daniel skulking around looking for a reason to *do something* about you two."

Laura scowled at the mention of Daniel. "You're right, of course." She kicked off her shoes and tucked her feet underneath her. She had spent hundreds of contented hours on Rhonda's tattered couch over the years, in that very position, hanging on the older woman's every word.

She used one hand to pet her dog and with the other brought the glass to her chin, inhaling the bergamot and lavender steeped tea. The typically soothing blend was doing nothing to abate her worries that night as she wondered if Sarah could somehow get a pass from Daniel's latest assignment.

"I wish she would talk to me, or anyone for that matter. Did you know she quit going to church?"

Rhonda had not known. "That's a shame. I bet Andrew would pull his heart out of his chest and hand it to her if she asked him for it."

On the way home, Laura detoured down a narrow dirt road that only a handful of locals would know about and even fewer would dare to go looking for. About a mile in, she slowed the Jeep, turned off the headlights, and pushed in the cigarette lighter. When it popped, she coaxed a tiny flame from the coil into one hand and took her .38 from the glove box with the other.

Hopping down, she called into the darkness, "Adira, are you there?"

She hoped that the mountain lion queen would be nearby, but there were a few portals, so if Adira didn't show up, Laura would hike Ford Canyon looking for her in the morning. Not only was a storm bearing down, but something much worse could have been lurking in the desert and she didn't want to linger by herself for long.

From behind the rocks, Adira watched her pace in the darkness. She could sense the spirit residue attached to Laura and flattened her ears in disgust. Though it was capable of causing plenty of damage, a brush with Tromluí could not guarantee anything other than the most random of results. After all, one person's nightmare could simply be another's casual memories.

Few from her realm would waste their time on such indeterminate magic and those beings weren't powerful enough to cross Sides. While the big cat was mildly curious as to who would want to attack the angel witch in such a way—and why—the exposure was something she couldn't reverse so she felt no need to mention it.

The shadows began to close in around Laura, but just as she stepped a foot up to the Jeep to leave, Adira emerged from the shadows flanked on each side by the Bobs.

In her head Laura heard, "You are brave to come here at this hour."

She had felt brave when she arrived, but no longer. Fortunately, Adira did not like to mince words so Laura quickly explained herself.

"Daniel told Sebastian that someone's trying to manipulate the portals between here and the Other Side," she was almost embarrassed to say it out loud, but added, "Andrew thinks a troll may be involved."

"Treats."

"Treats."

The small, sweet sound pushed through her mind and it took a moment for her to realize that it was the voices of the Bobs. They spoke one right after the other and flicked their stubby tails in anticipation.

She would have found it adorable if she didn't know they could kill her with a few swipes of their paws. She feigned offense and set her gun on the seat. "You know I wouldn't come to you empty handed." She poured some of Rhonda's bergamot syrup into an offering bowl and continued to their mistress, "Do you know what the guys are talking about?"

The cats were known to love syrup and though Adira abstained, the Bobs slurped it up. Instead, she scratched her claws in the sand and walked slow circles around Laura, making her nervous.

She stammered, "Is it true that...that both Sides can come and go as they please...through portals all over the world?"

"Assuming they can find one. Most importantly, there must be one available when they try to return home. It is dangerous to be trapped far away." Adira sniffed at Laura's knees and bumped against her hip. She reeked of the spirit and Adira conceded to herself that it was possible that the Tromluí could damage the witch's mind.

The thunder rolled closer, so Laura pressed. "Is there a troll in this area?"

"You've met him."

Laura curled her lip, "Richard."

"You cannot take on a troll while this is attached to you."

She looked down at herself in alarm. "While *what* is attached to me?"

"Use caution, Laura." Adira swished her tail and leapt up to the rocks above them, issuing a roar. The Bobs abandoned their syrup and followed close behind her.

"Good."

"Good."

"Ugh," Laura stared after them in confusion until a crack of thunder jolted her from her thoughts. She left the bowl of syrup and climbed into the Jeep; thankful she'd put the top on after Tina's party.

"I guess that was a waste of time."

Chapter Seven

"I'm home!" Adam tossed his keys on the counter and collected a water bottle from the refrigerator before finding Cara in their home office.

"You know, I believe Laura Deane has lost her mind." Her brows furrowed and Cara sat back from the computer screen as if it had just insulted her.

He doubted that she was serious but, the more he learned about the Deanes and their friends, it was low on the list of things that would have surprised him that night.

"She wants to sell her house and give Bash the money to help with expenses when she moves in with him. Can you imagine?"

He arched an eyebrow. "I don't get the impression that Sebastian Scott is the type of man who would take that money from her."

"You're right, he's old school for sure. But she wants to contribute and he won't talk about it, so she's come up with this hare-brained idea to sort of pre-pay for her bills."

He laughed. "That's really kind of sweet but at this point in his life, Laura being there is the only contribution he needs. I understand exactly where he's coming from," he pulled Cara's hair back and kissed her neck, "but you're right—at least we talked about those things before you moved in here."

"It's possible to do this while catering to both his hero complex and her independent streak, but I need to get them talking."

"I'm guessing it's been a long time since either one of them has dealt with this sort of thing. Was she ever married to the boy's father?"

"No," she snapped, and then hoped he didn't notice the change in her voice. She hadn't intended to be so short with him, but his question caught her by surprise.

He wasn't offended, but her tone fueled his curiosity. "Did he just run off?"

She pretended to study the screen. "Something like that."

Adam knew better than to press a woman who was obviously keeping another woman's secret and figured that ignorance would probably be bliss in that case. He dropped it and kissed behind her ear. "Are you coming out with me tonight?"

"I'll meet you later," she squeezed his hand and gave him a look, "and, I'll bring a blanket. Right now, I'm hoping to add the title of 'relationship counselor' to my resume."

Their one-eyed brindle Pitbull terrier waited patiently by the front door as Adam stuffed another water bottle into his backpack. "Come on Carl," he called.

They didn't typically leave Cara behind, so a

suspicious Carl hesitated until Adam led him back to the office where she snuggled and reassured them both before sending them off.

Evenings did not cool down during the hottest months of the summer and it was still easily ninety-five degrees outside with storm clouds hanging low, thickening the air. Lightning flashed ahead of him and he counted the seconds until the thunder cracked, realizing his outing would likely be cut short. The rain would feel good but Chuparosa was laced with dry washes and it would not do to get caught in a flash flood.

Adam took up the habit of late-night walks through town when he first moved in a couple of years earlier. Though no one tended to bother him, most folks who were out at that time weren't exactly headed to church. That's not to say he was, but he considered it a good idea for someone like him to keep an eye out for local threats.

Having grown up in Arizona, he was used to the desert and loved the mountains so he made it a sacred practice and eventually shared his favorite spots with Cara. No stranger to Chuparosa herself, she was able to fill him in on the finer points of the Other Side, inasmuch as one could do that.

The Other Side weighed heavy on his mind that night and he found himself searching for the natural bridge described by the men at the bar. It was just as they'd said: a little over a mile behind Laura's house, two large piles of rock wedged together in an arch, strangely ending just before it reached the dry riverbed. He found it unimpressive as far as landmarks went until lightning flashed and he glimpsed two goblins perched on the bridge and one skulking toward him along the bank of the river.

Carl barked viciously as the goblin inched closer to them and though his fighting days were mostly behind him, he could sense Adam's agitation and thrilled at the chance to protect his human friend.

Adam had been looking forward to telling Cara about the angel called Daniel and was disappointed when she chose to stay behind, but just then thanked Whoever was in charge that she wasn't there.

The goblin slashed the space in front of them with its claws and Adam dropped his fangs, crouching to meet the creature as it lunged. It leapt high and evaded Carl's mighty jaws, but Adam was fast and it screeched as he snatched it out of the air, twisting its head, and snapping its neck with a sharp pop.

"Hey, now." Lit up by the unceasing webs of lightning, the troll stood in the middle of the bridge flanked by the other two goblins with his long hair blowing loose in the wind. "Are you spying on me?"

"What do you want here in Chuparosa?" Adam called out. "What do you want with Laura Deane?"

"Why do you care about the angel witch? I've seen you out here with your own woman," his smile was smug, "wandering through the mountains in the hours before dawn."

He knew he shouldn't have been surprised, but it sickened Adam that other creatures had been casually observing some of his most intimate moments with Cara. "It sounds like you're the one spying on me."

"I know what you are," Richard sneered, "and you better mind your own business."

He called her an angel witch. Though Adam didn't yet

understand the full scope of their mission, the significance of what Chuck, Bash, and Drew had taken on was beginning to register with him. No matter what Daniel had charged them to do, if Laura and her sister were part angel but bound to the earth, they would be hunted by...everything.

The wind whipped across the riverbed, tearing branches from Mesquite trees and hurling Cholla cactus limbs through the air like spiked softballs. They could barely stand upright but the two goblins set out from their place at the troll's side, crossing the bridge to meet him. Carl hunkered in a defensive crouch next to Adam as they prepared to fight.

There were no more seconds between the lightning and thunder, and it crashed through the canyon with a sudden downpour of rain so hard that it stung their skin. The goblins could not fight the destructive force of the storm and had to skitter back to the bridge on all four limbs.

The rain blew sideways in gusts, blinding Adam. He and Carl could not withstand a microburst either, but before they ran, he called out to the troll, "Why do you want to make an enemy out of me?"

Running for the other side of the bridge, Richard looked over his shoulder and yelled, "I will come for all of you until I can make a friend out of Laura Deane."

* * *

Laura tossed in her bed as Tromluí's aura picked through her memories, splicing them into the darkest places of her mind. In murky light, she padded through the house of her childhood to the doorway of the bedroom Kevin shared with her mother. He leaned back in a rickety lawn chair positioned in front of the low dresser in the corner.

Growing up, Kevin was the man she'd known as her father. That was really all she'd ever known about the surly, self-righteous man and it turned out not to be true. In the mirror, she noticed that she wore her favorite off the shoulder sweatshirt and recalled that he'd thrown it away when he discovered it. *Slut.*

Kevin sat in front of the portable black and white television he'd taken from Laura and Sarah's bedroom. Though Miami Vice was on, he paid no attention to his favorite show. He was focused on his own reflection as he held a pistol to his temple, cocking and uncocking the hammer.

Her mother had once threatened, albeit with more dramatic flair, to kill herself with a pistol, but Laura found Kevin's quiet ritual much more disturbing. She'd seen it a handful of times, but never told Sarah, convinced it was better that only one of them was lying awake at night waiting for the blast if he finally pulled the trigger.

Moving from the doorway, she came across a toddler version of Brian setting up action figures on a blanket in the living room. A teenaged Sarah sat at the kitchen table sorting spices. Laura tried to go to them but bumped into a window of some kind. Pressing her hands against the glass in front of her, she observed that it ran the entire length of the room.

She jumped as the Brona demon emerged from the shadows, clomping hoofed feet and dragging sharp talons across the floor. Brian started to cry but Laura was blocked by the glass as she rushed to pick him up.

The demon prowled toward Sarah, who somehow could not hear the scraping of its claws on the tile.

Once more, Laura lurched forward but could not get to them so she pounded her fists on the glass yelling, "Sarah! Sarah! Look up!" But Sarah didn't move. Laura ran the length of the window until she was close enough to touch her sister, if not for the maddening barrier between them.

In desperation, she spun around looking for something to break it with, but behind her was only rotting wood framework. It dawned on her then that she was trapped within the walls of the house and she recoiled from the wood in horror, screaming and throwing her body against the glass.

A sudden blast startled her out of hysteria and her hands flew to her mouth as she realized it had come from Kevin's bedroom. The Brona demon scooped her crying child into its arms and, again and again, she threw herself against the glass, pounding her fists and screaming for her son.

When she woke, Laura's hair and nightgown were dripping with sweat, and she stood screaming and banging on her own bedroom window. Flustered and confused, she stumbled backward, tripping over pillows that had fallen off of the bed. She collapsed onto the floor, shaking and sobbing, and unable to control her breath.

Her phone startled her further with a text notification but even though she yelped again, she was grateful for the reality check. Crawling to the nightstand where it charged, she read that the message was from Cara Marshall, of all people, her friend and financial advisor:

C: I know it's late, but you didn't answer my
   email. Can we talk about this crazy plan you
   have for your house?

She did not want to talk about her finances and didn't want to wake Bash, who had to work in a few hours. She pulled her knees to her chest and selected the group text with Sarah and Audi, hoping one of them would still be awake.

L: Did you know the Bobs can talk?
A: whaaaaat

Her nerves calmed a bit after a brief back and forth with Audi about her latest encounter with the bobcats. Audi couldn't wait to hear them speak and her excitement lifted Laura's spirits, but she couldn't shake the heaviness of her dream. Since there was no response from Sarah, with fingers still trembling, she pressed Cara's number on her phone.

Chapter Eight

"Don't touch me!" The pain in Andrew's voice echoed through Sarah's mind in an endless loop. With her hands over her ears, she paced circles in the floor as if, somehow, she could block it out. She'd never lost control like that and was appalled that the man she loved was taking the brunt of her grief. She had no idea why she'd decided that the best course of action was to punish him but, since Rueben's funeral, she'd tried everything to cut Drew out of her life.

His feelings for her were no secret, but he'd never once acted on them. If she'd stayed with Rueben forever, he would have found a way to be content as her friend. He *was* a good guy and she'd mocked him for it. She let herself fall to the floor amidst the mess of boxes and rested her head on the couch cushion as sobs of shame consumed her. She was losing her mind and making a mess of everything that mattered.

When her tears finally slowed, she raised her head and settled her gaze on the picture of Fiona that Thomas had given them. She'd tossed it on top of a box of Brona's things that they'd cleared out of their mother's apartment after she died. Moving the picture to the floor, she dug her fingernail under the tape to rip open the box.

Poking through her mother's things, she realized that Laura must have put the box together. Another twinge of guilt tugged on her heart as she acknowledged that Laura had done nearly everything for Brona while Sarah hid behind Rueben. She made her husband a convenient excuse, even as he ignored her and as she wished he were someone else.

She shook off the fresh tears that threatened to flow and emptied the box, flipping through Brona's senior yearbook for a few minutes before setting it aside. *God, the woman was so beautiful on the outside.* There was her collection of dolls from The Wizard of Oz, minus the tin man that lived on Laura's kitchen windowsill, and a church cookbook that she'd put together to sell for charity. Notably, the box contained no photos of her daughters, but there were a few of Brian and Audi.

Laura had packed in a dozen or so of the books Brona collected about angels. They were all written by preachers and Sarah knew their perspectives were unlikely to have given her mother any comfort at all. If only she had asked to see Drew's collection of research. Sarah sighed to herself. *If only she told them anything about their lives.*

She choked back her rage and selected a more weathered book from the pile. Pieces of vellum and cardboard flaked off in her fingers and when she pulled on the ribbon that bound it, loose pages and dried flowers littered the floor as the binding fell apart in her lap.

"Do not disappoint me" was scrawled inside the front cover in handwriting she didn't recognize. Sarah was taken aback by the coldness of the inscription and then assumed it must have been written by Fiona. *Perhaps Brona was not the worst mother in the family.*

Most of the pages contained spells that Sarah recognized: basic protection, good luck, and healing. Each spell had comments written in the margins like, "too much mugwort," "cinnamon is better for this application," and "use your head, girl."

Was Brona being graded on her spells? There was a homemade throw pillow in the box and when she shoved it behind her against the couch, something inside of it poked Sarah in the back. She ripped the threads apart along one side and a smaller, homemade book fell into her lap. It was weak, but she could sense that a ward was wound into the braided ribbon holding it together. Brona had tried to protect the information in the little book, but not the one her mother graded. *Interesting.*

When they were teenagers, Sarah and her sister learned to create sigils from a book on numerology that Rhonda had given them. Each girl made her own for protection and to that day, they drew the symbols with their fingers on almost everything out of habit. Sarah took the magic marker she'd been using to label the boxes and drew her sigil on the ribbon. The cloth yellowed and unraveled, shrinking away from the cover and falling across her knees.

She flicked the ribbon into the box and opened the book to find that on the very first page was a hex. Sarah's head snapped back in amazement. She wondered which young girl had suffered Brona's plague of acne, and whether or not it had worked.

She turned the photo of Fiona over in her hands and found the name Vista Pines written on it. Well, not exactly written—Thomas had burned the inscription into the brown paper backing. *So dramatic.* A quick Internet search on her phone told her the general location of her grandmother's home in Flagstaff and she imagined it wouldn't be too difficult to find a witch in a trailer park.

Laura often joked that Brona had never spoken to them about their hellish heritage. She was only half-kidding, though, about the unfairness of being kept out of angel culture. Even if it meant learning about Thomas, they would have rather heard it from their mother. Laura believed they missed out on a close relationship because Brona was loathe to tell them about her past—their past. But as she pored over several more hexes and a handful of malicious 'love' spells, Sarah was intensely grateful that they hadn't learned a thing about magic from their mother.

A coldness gripped her as she glanced through the middle pages, and she looked to the ceiling for several minutes before allowing herself to continue reading. There in Sarah's hands, was the spell Brona used to summon an angel to guide her to a more mundane adulthood.

She had wanted a normal life, no doubt a life far away from Fiona, but she got Thomas instead. Kevin had no idea what she had done and according to the diary, by the time Brona tried to banish Thomas, she was already pregnant with Laura. She did not know how to banish the pieces of him growing inside of her child and Thomas threatened to kill her if she got an abortion. She and her sister were nearly two years apart and, stomach churning, Sarah wondered how her mother must have felt when he came back for her a second time.

The diary ended with some desperate ramblings about having done her part and vows to raise her wicked children in the church. Sarah knew the rest of the story all too well and she was done with her emotions for the night.

On a whim before setting the book aside, she flipped to the back and came across the heading, "When No One Should See." Even after reading the spell twice, she could hardly believe her eyes. Had her mother found a way to become invisible?

* * *

The New Sanctuary's congregation dwindled quite a bit when word got around that Pastor Clarke had teamed up with the Deanes to fight an evil of unclear origin. They weren't judging that his faith got messy, in fact, they were quite proud of him as long as they didn't get any of the mess on themselves.

The smaller crowd size allowed Drew to lead the more casual type of discussion that he preferred, even if it was looking on that Sunday like there wouldn't be more than two or three with him in the multipurpose room at the YMCA. He noted, uncomfortably, that Daniel was one of them.

He liked to think that his little church was a safe place to work through struggles in real time rather than a stage to make a show of unrealistic ideals. Drew kept himself casual as well, wearing dark blue jeans and a burgundy button down with the sleeves rolled to the elbows. The rich color of his shirt made his hair appear blonder and his eyes bluer, though they squinted with pain.

Chuck had been right and his whole body was sore but, as he rubbed at his neck, he knew his discomfort was more than physical. He wasn't surprised, but he still had to bite back his disappointment when it became clear that Sarah wasn't going to show up.

As the last person left, Daniel remained with his arm draped over the back of the chair next to him. Drew took that chair and folded it up. "Did you come to criticize?"

"I've been here before." Daniel was aware that his non-answer would irritate the preacher, so he helped Drew stack the remaining chairs, asking, "Why are they so anxious about what comes after death when life, here and now, can be so beautiful?"

Drew shrugged.

"It should be so easy," Daniel persisted. "You were put on earth to love and care for one another and given the tools to flourish as you do that."

"We've complicated everything over the years, or," Drew wondered aloud, "were early humans given more precise instructions?"

"Never," Daniel laughed, "the Watchers sought to help bridge the gap of understanding. In the end, they were probably right."

Drew's eyes widened at the admission, but Daniel cautioned him, "So much transcends our understanding, Andrew. Thomas wasn't punished because he disagreed. He was punished because he disobeyed."

"Was that his fate all along?"

"Humans are fated—not angels."

"At this point, I think fate is just another word for torture." Drew rubbed his temples. "Wasn't it fate that my father was a monster? I assume it was fate that I couldn't make babies."

Daniel shook his head. "Children had more to do with your ex-wife's future than yours."

"What are you saying?" Drew pressed his hand to his chest and leaned against the wall. "All that pain and anger? All that shame? You're telling me I was just a bystander?"

"Sometimes it works that way. She made her choices and the choices you made after that led you here."

Drew covered his face with his hands. "Holy shit, Daniel. I was so miserable for so long."

"But are you not the happiest you've ever been since coming to Chuparosa?"

Drew busied himself with slowing his heart rate and did not respond.

Daniel eyed the small wooden cross around the preacher's neck. "That's fine craftsmanship."

It had been a gift from his younger brother when Drew passed the Journeyman Electrician's exam. His brother had carved it himself out of a material Drew could wear on the job without risking electrocution.

"That brother died, did he not?"

Drew was unsure why Daniel wanted to bring up every horrible thing he'd ever gone through but hoped that he'd get some answers to some of his many questions if he cooperated.

"Drugs." He tucked the cross into his shirt, trying hard to keep his hands from shaking. "My parents thought they could beat the sin out of us, but I think that, in the end, they just beat out the sense."

Disheartened after his brother's death, Drew stopped wearing the cross. Then the angels he met left him reaching for answers that he felt were being held, unfairly, just outside of his grasp. They hadn't even given him any real proof of his god.

But the cross was a physical symbol he could touch, one that would ground him when his faith began to fall away. He decided to wear it again and Sarah had secured it to a new leather cord for him right before their battle with Thomas.

Daniel pushed that button as well. "No Sarah today?"

The back of Drew's neck tingled with warning. "She had some other things to take care of."

"You cannot afford to let the force of the Defenses diminish when one of the team strays from the path."

Drew pulled open the door to usher Daniel out. "I'll remember that."

A gust of wind blew the door inward as he pushed on the handle and Tromluí formed a cone of tiny crystals around Drew's body. "What the hell is that?"

"That is Tromluí." Daniel pulled him, gasping and coughing, out of the funnel and it whirled out the door. "It is a spirit of the night, nightmares, specifically."

"I've seen it before but it's so much bigger now." Drew caught his breath and remembered, "Thomas brought that thing to Tina's party last week."

"It's bigger now because the more of you it infects, the stronger it becomes. Andrew, you must prepare yourself for very bad dreams."

"Shit." he squeezed his eyes closed and recalled that Bash had told him of being attacked by the craziest dust devil he'd ever seen. "Can't *you* do something to help us?"

"That's not how it works. Even Thomas must have found someone else to summon it for him."

"Yeah, well you can tell God I've got some suggestions about how it works."

As if Drew had voiced the most idiotic notion, Daniel said, "No one sees God, Andrew," adding, "Michael is a Dream Master, and that spirit is from his realm, so I'll try to find him. In the meantime, you need to warn the others because no doubt Thomas has done this to immobilize you while he carries out some other plan. This will complicate your search for the shifting portal."

Drew slammed the edge of his fist against the wall. "Dammit."

* * *

At moonrise, Sarah dressed for the spell and the steamy August night in nothing but a white satin robe that fell just above her knees. Once, she'd worn it in an unsuccessful attempt to entice Rueben, but it had hung in the back of her closet since his rejection. He would have flat out guffawed if he'd seen her pull on hiking boots with it, but she couldn't go tromping through the desert without them.

She herself laughed at her reflection in the patio door glass as she hoisted a pre-packed tote bag onto her shoulder and stepped outside. The silky, thin fabric clung to her body as the humidity instantly dampened her skin.

August's full moon was a mere two days away and her path was lit with no need for a flashlight. She heard only the occasional scuttle in the bushes and the crunch of her steps in the sand as she approached her favorite spot. The area was scattered with large flat river rocks she'd long ago arranged in a pattern perfect for hours of meditation.

Spell work didn't truly interest her until recently, but she'd always used that space to work on her natural gifts, spending hours moving things around with her mind. There were times when she found herself overwhelmed by parenting her strong-willed daughter, and when she was sure the loneliness of her marriage would drive her mad. At her will, the smaller stones would rise to meet her and, plucking them out of the air, she would throw them into the canyon as hard as she could.

Over the years, when it became too much, she found a special kind of peace among those rocks and on occasions like that night, she used the unearthly place to practice more intense magic. She'd felt a slight violation of the space since they'd first encountered Daniel there but, smiling to herself, she knew what she was about to do would take it back for sure.

She unpacked the tote and lit a circle of white candles in the dirt, drawing a star in the center with salt. Brona's spell called for clear crystals, peppercorns, and lemon-lime soda, so she laid out quartz and a mason jar full of herbs and vodka. *Why not?* Brona was a teenager when she wrote the spell, but Sarah had adult experience and much more magical practice. She also had angelic powers that her mother lacked, so she'd added quite a few of her own embellishments.

She doubted there was enough angel blood in her to become truly invisible, but the main point of the spell was to deflect attention away. Young Brona hadn't thought of it, but Sarah set up five picture-sized mirrors facing away from her at each point of the star and placed a white throw pillow in the center of it.

She froze as a rustling came from underneath a nearby Palo Verde tree. Giant red ears poked up from underneath it and then she exhaled with relief, waiting for the rest of the jackrabbit to show itself.

"You might as well come on out."

It was not wise to venture in the desert without a sweet offering of some kind, so Sarah always had sugar cubes. Digging in the tote, she gathered a handful and held them out to her visitor, but the rabbit wouldn't budge.

"Still shy after all these years?"

She piled the cubes a few feet from the circle and went back to her business. The rabbit grinned with rows of sharp teeth and snatched up a cube, settling in to watch her perform the spell.

She slipped out of her boots, dropped the robe, and stepped naked into the circle—completely clean and unadorned, wearing no scents or makeup. A light breeze cooled her body when it touched the sweat on her skin and she sighed out loud at how good it felt. She settled down on the pillow and thought about how Laura would have loved to participate.

Yet another pang of guilt swept through her, but Laura had not been invited because Sarah had a plan that she was unwilling to drag her sister into. Pushing the feeling aside, she lit one more candle, held the crystal over the flame and uttered the incantation written by her mother over half-a-century earlier.

"Why do you wish not to be seen?" Sarah lifted her head to find Adira standing at the edge of her circle. She might as well have invited Laura since, apparently, everyone else was going to make an appearance.

"I'm going up north to meet someone and it may not be safe."

"Is it not dangerous enough for you here in Chuparosa?" Adira sniffed at the potion in Sarah's jar. "The magic in your line is strong and this spell should work well for you. Rueben's ghost will poison your travels though, as it has poisoned you against your family."

"I'm not against them," Sarah fumed, "I just need some time to myself. Why is that so hard for everyone to understand?"

Adira swished her tail and backed into the darkness, advising, "Let go of what haunts you before you leave, Sarah."

Sarah gulped down the potion and kept her eyes on Adira until she was sure the big cat was gone. The mountain lion was wrong. She missed her family desperately—she was poisoned against herself.

Daniel met Adira just outside the reach of Sarah's senses. "That one is increasingly unstable. My concern from the beginning was that the Deanes could not be trusted to stay the course of their mission."

"You mean your mission." She growled. "The Deanes are powerful allies, and it would be foolish of you to attack them now."

"It's unlike your kind to protect humans." He arched his eyebrows. "How is it that you care so much for that family?"

Her ears twitched in annoyance. "Do not confuse me with a pet. They keep their promises, and we require nothing of each other beyond an honest exchange."

"For that you bestow such loyalty?"

"For now, I am concerned only with what is fair."

"Your way is very cold."

"Is it?" She looked up at him with astonishment. "Tell me...why must humans be tormented so, before they can be blessed? At what point will this family have suffered enough for you and your master?"

Audi was just getting home from school when Sarah stepped quietly up to the back porch. She slipped her hand inside her robe, touching the clear crystal she'd wrapped in thin wire and hung from a chain around her waist. She held her breath just inside the sliding glass door as Audi reached past her and pulled it closed.

"I guess we're not even locking the doors these days." Audi muttered before grabbing an orange off the counter and heading to her room.

Sarah stood with one hand clutching the tote to her chest and the other over her mouth. *It worked.*

Chapter Nine

"Well, shit." Chuck snapped on the latex gloves Bash tossed him and knelt to prod at the ligature marks around the young man's broken neck. "That explains why we couldn't get in touch with him."

He and Bash had just taken statements from the two mountain bikers who came across the shirtless body.

"You guys can go—we'll be in touch if we need you." Bash said.

The bikers were happy to get away from their gruesome discovery and rode off at top speed.

Bash raised the back of his hand to his nose against the smell and frowned. "You would call this guy a ginger, right?"

Chuck paused while his partner crouched to inspect the young man's short, cropped hairline. "Talk to me, man. What don't you like?"

"Laura said the ranger they met had thick, long, gray hair. She said he wore a ponytail."

Chuck retrieved a file from his truck. "But this guy here matches the identification photo that the county sent us when they hired him, there's no question about it."

Bash turned the man's head from side to side. "There are no marks on this kid's face. Missy Trainor said she clawed up her attacker." He texted Laura a picture of the body, then called her on speaker mode.

"Gak, Sebastian don't send me random dead people like that. Jesus, I'm in Target."

"Sorry baby, I forgot you went to Phoenix today." He motioned for Chuck to pay attention to her, "So, you think that guy is random?"

"I don't know who that is." Worry crept into her voice, "What happened to him? Are you okay? What's going on?"

Chuck leaned over the phone. "We're on Willow Trail Laura, and that's the new park ranger, Richard Jeffries."

"What? No, that's not the ranger—not even close."

Drew rang in on Bash's second line. "I'm getting another call baby, and it'll take forever for the medical examiner to get out here. It's gonna be a long day, so call me when you get home."

For the most part, they could buy, make, or grow anything they wanted in Chuparosa, but every now and then the need would arise for a trip to Phoenix. When Laura was commuting downtown for work every day, any extra trips to the city were a hassle to be avoided and she tended to hunker down at home. But as a young retiree, she found herself looking forward to shopping trips and dates with Bash in town.

She thought about spending the night at his house,

but he was working late on the Jeffries case, and she'd been caught in rush hour traffic, so she picked up some of her favorite Indian takeout and headed home. Bash was not a fan of curry, and though she doubted he would deny her anything, she never suggested it and was looking forward to enjoying the rare treat with a glass of wine while she finished up a few projects.

That morning, she had dropped off a batch of her latest teas at a metaphysical shop she'd done business with for years. The proprietor was a good friend of Rhonda's and had been the first one to order from Laura's fledgling botanical business. Most of the shops she worked with had some sort of direct deposit for sales, but Wenona at the Off-World Owl still preferred to deal in cash, in person. After handing Laura a surprisingly fat envelope, she used a feather to push smoke at her from a bundle of sage that smoldered on the corner of the desk.

Wenona pursed her lips, "Girl, what have you gotten into now?"

"Hmm," Laura leaned into the smoke. "That's twice someone has claimed I have something on me that I can't see."

Wenona clipped the feather into Laura's long hair and sent her away with some supplies and plenty of advice that she hoped to make good use of that night.

Having been unable to shake off her nightmare about the house, she finalized a spell to minimize the intensity of any future dreams and sealed her work into several small jars.

Then she put together new shield bracelets for Bash and Drew, creating some for Chuck and Noah as well. Late into the night, she worked protection magic into the new obsidian shields, now threaded onto thick paracord that would close around their wrists with sturdy plastic clips.

Working on Bash's shield, she visualized him safe and happy, throwing his head back the way he did when he laughed, his cowboy hat barely hanging on. The magic flowed through her house and the technique was working so well that images of the man she loved began to flash in front of her.

Watching the scenes as they flickered through her kitchen, a sense of dread started working its way through her consciousness. She closed her eyes to push it out of her mind. A few deep breaths later, she opened them and jumped up from the table. No longer laughing, Sebastian was screaming, and he was in pain.

After doing his best to wash off the day, Bash flung his towel over the shower door and pulled on a pair of sweatpants. He would never be able to scrub the image of the young man's dead body from his mind but distracted himself with his reflection in the mirror. He plugged the sink and wrenched on the hot water, taking his aggravation out on the faucet.

He knew he was acting like a spoiled child, but he felt Laura's absence acutely that night. He'd hoped to have a more serious conversation with her about moving in and he wanted to talk about Andrew's warnings as well as the dead ranger.

Smearing a handful of shaving cream on his face and over his neck, he ruminated on how much easier and safer their lives would be if she lived with him and his mood soured further.

He studied himself for a bit and then, with a sigh, pulled the razor down the side of his face and swished it in the steaming water. He wasn't trying to look thirty years old, but he didn't want to look seventy, either.

After rinsing away his beard, he smoothed on some after shave gel and inspected the goatee he'd left behind for Laura. Reminding himself with a smirk where she liked the feel of his facial hair, he decided that the scruffy little bit of gray that remained would be fine.

Sitting bolt upright in bed a few hours later, his vision adjusted to the darkness, and he glimpsed a shadow hovering in the doorway of his bedroom. He jerked open the nightstand drawer, but his pistol wasn't there.

"Shit."

Jumping out of bed, he moved to follow the shadow as it flittered down the hallway. The bedroom door slammed shut behind him and he spun around, jerking on the handle, unsurprised that it was locked. He turned his back to it and found himself outside, in his yard.

He wiped his sweaty palms on what he thought was the t-shirt he'd fallen asleep in, but it turned out to be the camouflage uniform he'd worn almost every day for twenty years in the Army. Knowing it had to be a dream, he pinched over and over at the skin on his forearm but could not wake himself up.

Bash's fears were few, but Tromluí didn't have to dig deep to find them. He covered his head and ducked under the porch, grabbing a handful of rocks as a bloody faced harpy screeched and soared in circles around overhead.

"Bash!" He heard Chuck's call from across the yard.

His partner was also dressed in the desert camouflage and he was surrounded by goblins. Bash ran to him, throwing rocks at the creatures to draw them away. As he hoped, they started after him and he ran as fast as he could across the yard until to his left, he heard Laura screaming.

Her uniform, the same as theirs, hung two sizes too big on her body, making her appear helpless and small as she climbed up a fence, kicking at a revenant that had hold of her ankle.

"Light him up, baby!" He yelled. But her hands were bloody from the barbed wire and one slipped off, leaving her hanging by the other. Harpies circled them all, shrieking and chanting, but if he could avoid them for a few more seconds, he was sure he could get to her. As he neared the fence, one of the harpies alit in his path and grew until it towered over him. Bash fell backward in his tracks as vampire fangs lowered from the creature's mouth.

He gathered his courage and charged for it, but then the ground shifted underneath him, and his feet sank into the sand. He reached for anything he might use to pull himself out, but the sand was so soft and swallowed him so quickly that he didn't even get a final breath before it covered his head.

He woke violently, shouting and flailing his arms, knocking over the lamp and ripping his phone off the charger, sending it clattering under the bed.

He leapt up, sweat soaked and wild eyed, pacing in circles to calm himself down. He had such a hard time catching his breath that he thought his heart might thump right out of his chest. He flopped back on the bed clutching the pillow Laura slept on to his chest. The sheets had been changed since she was there last and the lavender vanilla combination he craved was gone. He hurled the pillow across the room, toppling everything on his dresser to the tile floor.

A clicking noise caught his attention and he realized it was his teeth chattering, so he pulled off his wet t-shirt and grabbed one from the dirty laundry hamper. It was one she had worn, and his mind began to clear as, at last, he could smell her against him.

Drew had warned him of a bad dream, but he never expected it to seem so real. Opening the nightstand drawer, he exhaled with relief, collected his pistol, and flipped on every light from the bedroom to the kitchen.

His hands shook as he poured himself a glass of water, spilling most of it on the floor. The clock on the microwave said 1:26 a.m., and though he didn't want to worry her by calling, he couldn't get the image of Laura climbing the fence out of his mind. He made his way to the living room and sank onto the couch, giving the coffee table a kick. It was just a dream but if she had been there, he would know for sure that she was safe.

The doorbell rang and once more he nearly jumped out of his skin. Still holding his gun, he cracked the blinds on the window to peer outside, rested his forehead on the wood frame in disbelief, then looked again.

There stood Laura, wearing running shorts and his sheriff's department sweatshirt. *That's where it went.* But for the overnight bag on her shoulder and Watson standing next to her, it was as if he'd wished her right out of bed.

On the other side of the door, Laura swallowed hard. Now that she was standing there, she began to feel stupid, but the vision had been so clear. She'd heard him cry out in her mind, and he hadn't answered his phone, so she was sure that something was wrong.

Though it was late at night, the sweatshirt she wore was inappropriate for the heat. Even so, she tugged at the fleece more from her nerves than the humidity and flinched when he opened the door.

"Holy shit, baby." He lowered his gun and pulled her across the threshold. "What are you doing here?"

He turned her hands over in his, inspecting them for cuts. They were as soft as ever, manicured perfectly with phosphorescent polish on the tips of her fingernails.

Her eyes welled with tears. "I...I felt..." She took the gun from his hand and laid it on the coffee table, "Bash, you were in pain."

"It was just a dream," he pulled her to him, "an awful, awful dream. Drew tried to warn me but I guess I didn't fully understand what he meant."

"Drew tried to warn you?" She pulled away, confused.

"He said Thomas put something on us that causes nightmares."

"Damn him." She dug a horseshoe out of her bag and tossed it in the fireplace. "I assumed our dreams were due to excessive monster exposure." She grinned through her tears. "Goblins and demons and harpies, oh my..."

"Yep, they were all there."

Her smile faded and she handed him a spell bottle. "The horseshoe will keep out the boogeyman and we can bury this in the yard tomorrow. It probably won't stop the dreams, but it should limit the damage they can do. I have one for each of..."

She'd wandered through the house while she was talking and stopped short at the doorway to his bedroom, which looked as if it had been ransacked.

He ignored her worried stare. "You didn't say you were having nightmares too. Why didn't you call me?"

She picked up the pillow in front of the dresser, tossed it on the bed and began to right the things that had fallen over. "Well, do you feel like talking about yours?"

"No." He selected a fresh set of sheets from the trunk at the end of his bed and slammed it closed.

"Wait, how did you feel me from three streets away?"

She shrugged. "I can sense the people I love the most, Bash. You know that."

He did know that, but until then he hadn't been completely sure he was still on the list.

When his room was put back together, she touched his face and smiled. "You shaved."

"I feel less like ole Santa Claus now."

She put her arms around his neck. "The sexiest Santa I ever saw."

Since seeing her on his doorstep he'd felt like a bit of a nuisance, having somehow summoned her in the middle of the night, but still he let her shower him with affection. Her head on his chest lowered his blood pressure and gave him a feeling of peace.

It was a feeling so strong that he often craved it like it was a drug. He was neither ready to go, nor did he harbor the delusion that he would get his wish when the time came, but that's how he wanted to die.

105

Chapter Ten

She woke to find him in the kitchen frying up eggs and bacon. Wrapping her arms around his middle, she asked, "Are you feeling any better?"

He handed her a plate. "That depends." He fed Watson a piece of bacon as they sat down at the table. "Are you going to move in with me or not?"

She was taken aback. "Do you think I don't want to?"

He pushed his eggs around his plate. "It's embarrassing now that I'm saying it out loud," His hair fell across his eyes, and he looked up with a sheepish smile, "but I thought you'd be a little more excited about it."

She squeezed his hand. "I am excited, but I'm nervous too. We need to talk about the details."

His phone rang and he stood up from the table. "It's Becky. Listen, I told you I'll take care of the details—just pick a date and we'll make it happen. Hey, Beck..."

Bash was one of those people who paced when he talked on the phone, absently picking up and setting down random items as he walked through the house. For that conversation, he selected a tissue box and swung it at his side as he spoke to his daughter.

"What? No kidding...Masters at NAU? Oh, I'm so proud of you, honey. You know Laura's boy, Brian, is up there? He's a senior, just a year younger than you." He put down the tissue box, ran a hand through his hair and picked up the box again, speaking a bit quieter. "Yeah, we're back together. I know...I know I should have listened to you all along."

Laura smiled into her coffee cup wondering what in the world those conversations must have been like. She glanced at the college graduation photo of Becky on the wall. It had been a terribly awkward event with Becky's grandmother scowling the whole time and refusing to speak to them; but, Bash was as proud of his budding relationship with his daughter as he was of her getting a degree.

He put the box down to give Watson some attention, then picked it up again. "Since you're in Arizona, do you think I could see you? What about Christmastime? Or is that...oh, yeah, I guess you're right. Grandma wouldn't understand...okay."

He closed his fist and crushed the tissue box into cardboard shards, but never changed his tone of voice with her.

"What can I do to help with school? You know I've—I've been saving all this time...alright sure...don't forget to send me that invoice. I know you gotta run. I love you so much, Beck...okay bye."

* * *

Fiona wasn't quick enough to catch the teacup when the blonde girl slumped down to the grubby floor, but as it turned out, the cheap linoleum had enough bounce in it that the cup remained undamaged.

It also turned out that while young girls entering the university were indeed adventurous, they were likewise willful and, to Fiona's vexation, highly suspicious.

After struggling to find the number of girls necessary for her healing coven, she was forced to change her tactics and she'd resorted to the one thing she swore she would never do. She placed an advertisement in the local paper pretending to be an elderly woman in need a part-time companion. Her ad requested someone with a good attitude who was willing to clean.

She acknowledged that the ad was vague and that she had no intention of paying anyone who came to her door, but Fiona couldn't understand why so few had applied for the position. *Was there no such thing as a starving student anymore?*

If the blonde's theatrical display was any indication of how other girls were going to react when Fiona told them of her predicament, she would have to forego future explanation of the coven and force the potion into them right away.

It had been messy but, at last, the manipulation spell worked its way through the young girl's mind as her body lay unconscious. Willing participants would have lessened the risk of official attention, but Fiona would have to take her chances and move quickly.

"When you meet our angel, you'll rethink everything, lassie."

Thomas had inadvertently encouraged her change

in mindset. No potion would be strong enough to get six women to Chuparosa, and even if it were, she would require their energy and intention for the healing spell. As it was, she couldn't even get their cooperation, but perhaps she could enlist the aid of her granddaughters.

Tromluí would make them weak and vulnerable, but most importantly, it would make them hate Thomas and they'd be more likely to help her with the spells necessary to turn him into her servant. If they were as strong as he said, Fiona might begin again in Chuparosa with improved health and more power than she'd ever had at her disposal.

One more girl would be enough to support her journey to the valley, and Fiona would contact her the next day. The voicemail had been garbled when she called about the ad, but her name was Rebecca. Rebecca Stewart, or Schott, or something like that.

* * *

Laura perched on the wooden fence railing in Bash's back yard while he dug a hole to bury her dream protection spell. Drew had stopped by, and she clipped a new shield bracelet onto his wrist as he leaned against a post explaining what he'd learned about Tromluí.

"Some say that dreams are just our brains taking out the trash, but this thing pulls pieces of our worst fears and memories to the forefront of our minds." He paled as he recalled screaming himself awake only hours earlier, causing Daphne, his cat, to leap off the bed and hide for hours in the corner.

He was seventeen years old again in his dream, being dragged through the church by two deacons. His father stood near the baptismal, still holding the belt he'd used to beat down his son before they left the house.

"This is for your own good." One of the deacons whispered in his ear.

He'd been weakened and demoralized, but as they neared the pool, Drew fought them with fresh energy, shouting, "It was just a concert!"

"That's the devil in you," his father motioned for the deacons to lower him into the water, "no son of mine will be seen at Satan's theater ever again."

Drew struggled to climb out, but his wet hands slid down the walls of the pool as they pushed him under. Blood from the belt lashes on his back oozed around him, turning his vision red as the water covered his face.

Fighting for each gulp of air, he could hear only muffled words from his father's reading and the echoes of his own fists pounding against the walls of the pool. Until the moment he woke up, he never lost sight of the belt dangling loosely underneath the Bible in his father's hand.

Young Drew understood baptism to be a public promise to follow the church and what it perceived to be God's law. He was doing no such thing that day and became convinced over time that the forced baptism had somehow damned his soul.

Laura touched his cheek "Drew?"

Bash held up his wrist to show off his new shield bracelet. "He must be upset because I got the special left-handed version."

Drew shook off the memory and the dream, grateful for Bash's teasing. "I'm afraid that you, too, my southpaw friend, would have been burned as a witch back in the day."

"Yeah, well," Bash leaned on the shovel, "it's always something with me."

"Anyway," Drew continued, "the spirit is doing the will of whoever summoned it and our brains are just trying to process the intrusion, so we don't go mad."

Bash sneered. "Thomas."

"Remember, angel powers are limited too. Daniel said that Thomas would have needed someone else to summon it for him."

"A witch." Laura put her hand to her forehead, "I bet that's why he went looking for Fiona."

"But that woman has to be in her eighties or nineties by now."

Bash knelt and piled some rocks over the dirt mound. "We can't afford to be naïve about this. He has us off balance and you know it's just a distraction for something worse.

Laura frowned, scratching at her skinned knees. "I think it got me when I fell on the trail, the day we met Richard."

Drew squeezed Bash's shoulder. "I'm pretty sure it got you twice. Didn't it bump you at the party after Tina opened the box?"

Bash stood and wiped his hands on his jeans. "Lucky me."

"What Thomas doesn't realize is that this Tromluí will have to work a lot harder to scare me with a dream." Laura said, pursing her lips, "Has he forgotten that I made my own demon?"

Whether she was truly afraid or not, Drew worried that Laura spent a lot of time making magic to protect the rest of them, but seemed to accept certain things that happened to her, almost as if she deserved them. If Adam was right and the troll was after her, he would somehow need to make her understand the danger while keeping Sebastian calm about it.

"There's something else," he warned, "Adam said he came across a man in the desert the other night at the natural bridge. He wore a parks and rec uniform with Richard's nametag on it, but you said the real Richard Jeffries is dead."

Bash stabbed at the dirt with the shovel. "He literally took the shirt off that kid's back."

"Based on what Adam said, this guy's not human, so he's probably our troll. We should assume he at least knows about what's going on with the portals, and," Drew kept his eyes on Bash for a reaction, "he thinks he has business with Laura."

Unfazed, she rubbed her hands together and pulled some static electricity out of the air, curling it around her fingers for them to see. "This will work even better when the air is dryer this winter."

Bash said nothing, but his knuckles on the hand that gripped the shovel were completely white.

Drew hung his head. *Zero success on both counts.*

"There you are, Auntie!" Audi and Noah rushed around the house. "I've been trying to get in touch with you for an hour."

Laura put her hand to her empty back pocket and realized her phone was still on the kitchen table. The younger two rolled their eyes in irritation and Audi asked nervously, "Have you heard from my mom?"

"Maybe she left me a message." Laura exchanged looks with the men and followed Audi into the house.

Noah winced as Bash hauled himself onto the fence.

"Dude, your joints sound like bubble wrap."

"Shut up, punk." Bash gave him a playful shove. "This is your future, especially if you keep hanging out with us."

Noah looked hopeful. "Are you inviting me along?"

Drew chuckled, "That would be a terrible idea son, but just in case…" he pulled one of Laura's shield bracelets out of a small pouch she'd left on the fence and tossed it to him. "Don't take it off."

Noah proudly clipped it on, but his expression sobered a bit when he felt the power surge around him.

"No message." Laura returned shoving her phone in her back pocket in a dramatic display for Audi's benefit. "We're going to search the trails by Sarah's house. It's not unlike her to lose track of time out there."

Audi kicked at the dirt. "Yeah, but she would go apeshit if I ignored her like this."

Bash turned to Drew. "Go with them. I'm gonna see what me and Chuck can dig up on Fiona Deane."

Noah had been trying hard to take Bash's advice, but Audi was wound up even tighter than usual on that day, so he resorted to impersonating the man outright.

"I have to go on shift…baby." He was disappointed that he had to leave them, and worried about her. "Please be careful out there."

She walked him to his truck and Drew laughed again. "I think you're the object of some hero worship, Sheriff."

Bash frowned. "Speaking of terrible ideas…"

* * *

"Hello, this is Rebecca Scott…"

Brian's head jerked up in recognition of the name. He never listened that carefully when his mother talked about the sheriff, but he'd thought the man's daughter lived back east somewhere. It probably wasn't her, but the tedium of the morning was wearing on him and he became curious anyway.

He'd been waiting in line over half-an-hour for his turn at the Bursar's office window in hopes of sorting out his scholarship funds. He had the same problem every semester: the funds were transferred directly to the school, so Brian had to beg the school to get the money for his books and other expenses.

The rules of the scholarship and the demands of the swim team and his studies meant that he couldn't hold down a proper job. Though he earned a fair amount of money as a math tutor, his mother supplemented his cost of living and paid for his meal plan.

It was a situation he could hardly stand anymore but since he knew she would never let him pay her back, he vowed that she would not want for anything in her second half of life.

She'd once jokingly requested a nursing home with only hot male orderlies and Brian wondered to himself if that were the sort of thing old ladies included in their Yelp reviews. In any case, he planned to do plenty of research when the time came.

Rebecca was in line, two people ahead of him, and he continued to eavesdrop on her conversation.

"Vista Pines? I'm not familiar with the area, but I have GPS. What number? Ok, I'll be there for the interview at 4 p.m. Thank you for your time."

Vista Pines? *Gross.* What kind of interview could she

possibly have in that place? Brian leaned a bit closer when she reached the window. A collective groan issued from the others in line as it became clear her issue was just like everyone else's. The university had no record of whatever it was that had most definitely been done.

She gritted her teeth with a temper barely controlled. "No, I already told you..."

"Hmph, where have I seen that attitude before?" Brian muttered to himself.

"My father paid the invoice. It's probably under the name Sebastian Scott." She pulled out her phone. "Here, let me show you. He emailed me the receipt."

The kid at the counter said they would research it and Brian watched her as she found a seat. By that time, there was no doubt in his mind that the young woman was the sheriff's daughter. Rebecca was tall like her father and had his rich brown eyes. Her hair was a lighter caramel-color than his, falling unrestrained in long natural waves down her back.

Having at last resolved his own issue, morbid curiosity got the better of him and he found her, still fuming, in her seat.

"Excuse me," he said, and though she gave him an 'I dare you' look, he hoisted his backpack higher onto his shoulder and said, "I swear I'm not creeping here, but you said Sebastian Scott is your father. Did you mean Sheriff Sebastian Scott?"

She leapt to her feet and just before she turned on her heel to leave him, he patted his chest and added, "I'm Brian Deane—Laura's son."

Chapter Eleven

Watson rolled in the dirt as if trying to absorb the magic that crackled around Sarah's special place in the desert.

"She was out here, and not that long ago," Laura poked a stick at what remained of the white candles in the fire pit. "But I don't know what she's been working on."

They looked to Audi for an answer, but she rolled her eyes. "What? Other than another bottle of wine?" Her lip trembled when Drew looked away. "I know what she did to you, Pastor Clarke."

That thought horrified him and he shook his head, "Audi, please don't..."

"She wrote about it in her journal, and she wants to take it back so bad," her voice cracked, and she sobbed, "yeah, I read about it, and I guess I'm a horrible person, but she left it open on the couch." Tears spilled down the young woman's cheeks. "Your fight is the last entry and that's all I read; I swear."

Laura didn't know what had happened between Sarah and Drew, but she knew that both her sister and her niece needed help. Watson nuzzled at their knees as she hugged Audi tight. Somehow the dog seemed to understand that Audi had been kidnapped, she'd lost her father and had been watching helplessly as her mother unraveled. Laura fought hard to hold back tears herself. So much was always happening to all of them, and it was happening so fast that they were beginning to fail each other.

Drew pulled them both into his arms. "Audra, concern for your mother does not make you horrible."

"Besides," Laura said matter-of-factly, "I'd have read the whole damn thing." They laughed at Audi's surprise but as an only child, she wouldn't have understood how few boundaries most siblings were willing to observe.

"No one knows how they'll react in a situation like hers until it happens." Laura defended Sarah, adding, "It's not the same, but don't forget that you have us, too."

They hiked along the bank of the dry riverbed, then around the base of the butte until they came upon the natural bridge. Dark monsoon clouds were rolling in from the edge of town and though the forecast said Chuparosa wouldn't see any rain from those clouds, it was like walking around in a wet furnace. Drew took off his baseball cap and wiped his brow. "Your house is just over there?"

Laura nodded and took a long drink from her pack. "I'll drive you both home because we've hit a wall out here."

"Hey, now," Richard hopped down from the side of the bridge and advanced on them.

Laura and Watson spun toward the voice, her

fingers already charging with electricity.

"That's him." Audi whispered to Drew.

Richard waved his finger at them. "Didn't I say you'd come back to me?"

"Who are you, really?" Drew asked.

"I don't have a name that you can comprehend but, Richard was a nice enough fellow so, I'll stick with that—in his honor, as it were." Watson barked a warning, but Richard was unafraid. His eyes hardened and he took Laura by the arm. "It's time to go across."

As her dog leapt at him, Laura jerked away, and Drew threw a punch across his jaw. Richard's head snapped back but he recovered quickly, lifting Watson off the ground by his collar and Drew by his shirt.

"This is not about you." He snarled.

As he shook them, Drew's cross fell across the back of Richard's hand and burned itself into his skin. He roared in pain and tossed them aside, turning his attention to Laura.

Drew rolled onto his knees, held Watson back with one hand and pulled out his pistol with the other, firing a shot into the troll's shoulder.

Richard's legs buckled but he didn't go down, so Laura pushed a handful of electricity into his chest and Audi swept her arms overhead, knocking him backward over a pile of rocks.

Richard held one hand to his shoulder and reached for her with the other. "I have no reason to hurt you just yet, but you're coming with me."

Laura gathered her family to her and wrapped a static shield around them. "Like hell I am."

Richard spit on the ground in front of her and hobbled back across the bridge. "One way or another, bitch, you will hear what I have to say."

* * *

On the drive up to Flagstaff, Sarah brooded over Adira's comments. For months she'd convinced herself that she was consumed with guilt over the manner of Rueben's death. It was true that she relived the landslide that took his life over and over and, in her dreams, she still pushed the rubble away from his lifeless face. But if she were being honest, his death only brought to the forefront all the other ghosts that had haunted her for years.

At the Sunset Point Rest Area, she leaned against the guardrail, staring for a long time into the valley below the Bradshaw Mountains. She had to admit that more than guilt, it was anger and regret she'd been wrestling with for all those months. She didn't regret getting married and their child would always be the true love of her life, but she did regret giving up on her happiness.

As the disappointment crept in over the years, how could she have felt so little regard for her youth that was being sacrificed along the way? She was angry with herself for doing nothing to force a change in her marriage. Even as night after night her husband slept with his back to her, she would not admit that they had failed and certainly not that she deeply loved another man.

She wrapped her hands around the guardrail and squeezed until her fingers went numb. She was unsure that she would have ever found the courage to reshape her future if Rueben hadn't died and *that* is what filled her with shame.

She didn't necessarily feel any better by the time she stopped for gas in Munds Park, but her head was clearer. The air temperature in northern Arizona was still warm but the breeze was cool—a delightful change from the stifling hot winds in Chuparosa.

A nagging worry for her sister was settling in at the edge of her mind but, thankfully, the banshees were leaving her alone, so she allowed the fresh smell of the pine trees to calm her and sent Audi a text:

```
S:  Check on your auntie
A:  k
```

Sarah found her grandmother easily enough and the kind man in the trailer park office was exceedingly grateful for the ointment she gave him.

Since starting her botanical business, Laura had been experimenting with potions and teas that were not likely to ever be sold to the public and she'd given all the witches she knew a pouch full of magic that they carried with them everywhere.

The man swore the angry red welts were just gnat bites, but Sarah had never seen anything like it.

Because of her help, he didn't bat an eyelash when she asked about Fiona, and Sarah was peering through her dirt smeared kitchen window within minutes. She was surprised to also see a young woman busy at the stove and another one stuffing wadded up clothes in a suitcase on the couch.

Footsteps approached from down the lane, and she touched the crystal around her waist just before an old, fiery headed woman tromped up the walkway through the puddle at the foot of the steps. Sarah clapped her hand over her mouth to keep from gasping aloud. But for her height, Fiona could be Laura travelling through time.

Inside, the old woman barked orders and the younger ones sat down quietly at the kitchen table. She ladled out a bowl of whatever was in the pot and then emptied in the contents of an envelope pulled from the pocket of her skirt.

To Sarah's annoyance, but not her surprise, Thomas alighted on the front porch and barged through the door.

Fiona handed him the bowl and though he took it from her, his tone was ungrateful and harsh.

"Your Tromluí has failed, witch. They're supposed to be delirious and distracted but I would say they're no more than a bit uneasy."

"It's not my fault that their real lives are scarier than their nightmares. What kind of father are you anyway?" She pointed at the bowl. "Eat yer soup." She handed him a spoon after he slurped some off the top. "Not like an animal."

"It makes my life more difficult—not to mention yours." He took the chin of one of the women at the table. "There are not many small-town sheriffs who will just let you march in with two kidnapped girls and perform a dangerous ritual. This cowboy in particular will be hell bent on making himself a menace to your logistics."

She gave him a joyless smile and tried to ignore his loud slurping. "What *are* the logistics anyway?"

"There's an abandoned train yard just south of town, and that area is pulsing with energy from both Sides of the veil. You can hole up there with your *assistants* until your ritual is completed. Then you'll have to give back the girls and hope that Laura can be reasonable about the whole business."

As he lifted his spoon, a deafening crack echoed through the forest. Thomas guarded his soup while ducking away from items that flew from Fiona's shelves as the trailer nearly vibrated off its concrete blocks. Fiona's eyes widened and she pressed her hands to her chest, knowing in her bones that they had just heard a witch's death knock. The first of three.

Outside, Sarah stifled a screech and used her arms to protect her head from the pinecones raining down from above. Once the tremors settled, she returned to the window to find Thomas mocking as Fiona's face twisted with desperation.

"Tick tock," he jeered.

With two more death knocks to come, there was still time, but not as much as she'd hoped. Fiona gathered her composure and ladled more soup into his bowl, allowing her expression to turn haughty as he dug in.

"As I was saying, Laura will..." He stopped speaking and listed toward the counter, shifting his gaze from Fiona to the bowl with sudden outrage.

"Laura's gonna do exactly what I tell her to do, and so will you...angel."

Outside, Sarah stiffened. Was that woman actually trying to cast a spell on an angel? She raised her arm and used her mind to knock the bowl from Thomas's hands. The contents sizzled when they hit the floor and he fell backward grabbing at his throat, rasping, "Are you insane?"

"Possibly," she shrugged, "but I've lost a lot more than a healthy body over the years and your...*our* family is gonna help me get it all back."

Thomas' vision blurred and he croaked in disbelief, "No...no you can't."

"Relax, it's just a mild poison. It'll keep you down while I work the spell." She tilted her chin up proudly, "I only made it a li'l bit stronger than the one I used on them." She tugged on the hair of one of the girls who then jumped up and collected a small wooden box from Fiona's room.

Thomas lurched toward the door, slumping against it until Sarah jerked it open, pulling him out and into the mud. The fresh air revived him slightly as he stumbled toward the woods but, though he spread his wings, he was unable to fly. Sarah followed until he collapsed a few hundred feet away from the trailer park, then she sank to her knees at his side.

"Thomas!" She slapped his face to wake him. "Thomas what have you done?"

His jaw went slack as Fiona's venomous intentions fueled the poison coursing through his body. Sarah searched in the pouch Laura gave her for something to slow the spread and opened his mouth to let a few drops fall onto his tongue. "I don't know if this will work on idiot angels or not."

He didn't move, so after a few moments, she poured in the entire vial. "Here goes nothing."

She leaned against a tree, unsure of the protocol if he died. Would he disappear? If not, what did one do with a dead angel's body? While she wished Daniel had given them a way to contact him, Thomas began to sputter and twitch. He rolled over to his hands and knees so, satisfied that he would survive, she touched the crystal on her waist and backed away.

Gagging and swearing, he called after her, "Sarah! Come back here...Sarah!"

Chapter Twelve

Laura put on her new dress and studied her reflection in the mirror. She preferred dresses, particularly in the summertime and had ordered three from a friend with a shop in Phoenix. The one she selected for that night was a simple, royal blue, v-neck with a white hem that fell just above her knees. She paired it with flat, white, canvas sneakers and a crescent moon that hung from a silver chain around her neck.

A new dress always gave her a confidence boost, even a casual dress, and she really needed the boost that night. It irritated her, but she was terribly insecure about her future living arrangements and Bash was as unhelpful in that regard as he could be. Even so, she couldn't wait to see him and looked forward to some uninterrupted time together as they discussed their future.

She left the bedroom and flipped off all the lights except for the one in the kitchen and lit several candles throughout the living room. She could feel her stress level lower as the soothing, soft glow permeated the space. Settling down on the floor next to the coffee table, she shifted her thoughts from Bash to the conversation she'd had with her sister that morning.

Sarah had been insistent. "I'm going to Flagstaff to meet Fiona."

"You're walking into a trap."

"It's not a trap if I'm ready for it and I'll even check in on Brian. Let me do this, Lolly. I need to do this."

The clouds were thick, but it looked as if the forecasters were right, and nothing would come of them except more humidity. Still, Watson paced a trail though the house, back and forth between her spot in the living room and the kitchen patio door. "Don't worry sweet boy," she tried to soothe him, "no weather tonight."

It was not the weather that had Watson spooked. Outside, Richard was searching for a weak spot in her wards as he stalked the perimeter of her house. He was determined to bring back the angel witch, but his power diminished the farther he travelled from the bridge. Though he was only a couple of miles away from home, he didn't want to risk using too much of his own power on details like getting past her magical security.

She was well protected, but he'd come with a gift from his benefactor. He dipped his finger in a small jar, coating it with a silver liquid he then used to draw symbols on the exterior walls of the house.

Inside, Laura shuffled the papers in front of her. Cara had suggested putting together some information in writing for Bash to look at. She felt that a visual representation of Laura's concerns would lead to a more productive conversation about moving in together.

When he called just then, the sound of his voice made her smile.

"Your grandmother has led quite a life. She's practically notorious in wealthy Flagstaff circles, always just this side of theft and suspicious accidents."

"Why am I not surprised?" she quipped.

"Something bad must have happened because now she lives in a shitty trailer park on the outskirts of town."

Laura grew more anxious. "Sarah found it and is on her way there."

"Damn her," Bash swore. "You guys were torn up in the desert while she was on her way to the mountains. Come over, baby—I want to see you."

"I was hoping you would come here. I want to show you some things."

"See how much easier this will be when you live here full time?"

"That's what I want to talk about."

Bash was angry with himself for not being there when Richard attacked and couldn't keep the frustration out of his voice. "God, it doesn't have to be this complicated."

She had worked hard to keep any reservations about moving in with him to herself and was losing patience with his unwillingness to address even the most basic logistics with her. "Why are you acting like this? I'm just trying to do things right."

"Well, dammit woman," he snapped, "I'm just trying to love you."

He ended the call and tossed his phone onto the couch while she stared at her own phone in disbelief. Why was he being such an asshole? Why was it always so hard when they both wanted exactly the same things? She moved her thumb over the green button under his name but thought better of it. It would do no good to talk while they were angry and tired. She looked down at her 'confidence' dress and laughed out loud.

The silver in the symbols Richard had drawn all over the house lit up as he muttered the words that would dismantle Laura's wards. A wave of vulnerability washed over her then and the plant on the coffee table wilted in its pot. She jumped up and unlocked her phone but hesitated in shock as every other plant in the living room wilted around her. "Oh..."

Richard ripped the casing off the electrical box affixed to the house and yanked out the wires. When the kitchen light went out, Watson ran to the glass door barking ferociously and Laura held her breath to fight back her fear. "...shit."

She scooped the flame from one of the candles and went to the kitchen where Watson jumped and scratched at a shadow crossing the patio. Before she could make sense of what was happening, Richard crashed through the glass.

"Hey, now," he grabbed her wrist and snatched her phone away, tossing it out the door. Watson lunged and latched his jaws underneath the intruder's arm, but Richard spun and slammed the dog against the wall over and over until the bite loosened enough that he could fling him away.

Laura screamed, "Watson!" and sent a bolt of fire into Richard, pushing him out the door. She followed him to the porch and released another stream of fire, but he raised his hands and deflected it into the pots of herbs behind him. "I'm ready for you this time, witch."

He charged at her, pushing her body backward. They crashed into the wooden beams of the pergola then smashed down on the planter containing her favorite rosemary bush.

She staggered to her feet, rubbed her hands together and wrapped his head in a web of static electricity. He bellowed in pain and reeled away, grabbing her by the shoulders and using his weight to shove her body against the house while he pulled a knife from his belt and held it under her chin.

"It didn't have to be this way," he said, "but you're so stubborn." He threw her down on the wooden worktable and pinned her there, then held her hand out and slid the blade of the knife across her palm. "Maybe you'll think twice before burning me next time."

As she kicked and screamed, Watson bit down on Richard's leg. He lost his grip on Laura but shook his leg away and kicked the dog across the porch and under the grill, which toppled over, trapping Watson underneath.

Laura rolled off the table to the terra cotta tile, and as she tried to crawl toward the house, Richard picked up the table and threw it, blocking the doorway. She tried to pivot away but he grabbed her by the hair and jerked her to her knees.

"You'll have to kill me now," she panted, "because I'm not going with you."

He raised the arm bloodied by Watson's bite and backhanded her across the face. Her vision tunneled as her head hit the tile and the porch began to spin around her. Just before her eyes closed, she heard him say, "I'll kill you when I'm good and ready to."

Bash immediately felt like shit after hanging up on her and swore at himself as he dug for his phone between the couch cushions. He swore again when she didn't answer his call. *Stubborn woman.*

His tone turned apologetic though when her voicemail came on. "Laura...baby, I'm sorry. I'm coming over."

He used his key when she didn't answer the door and, peeking around the entryway, he hollered, "It's Bash...I let myself in so don't shoot me god dammit...you were right, okay? Let's talk about this."

He picked up one of the papers strewn on the coffee table. In the candlelight he could see that she'd drawn a map of his back yard, diagraming where her plants would go. She'd written little notes in the margins of the page about the best sunlight and where they should put shade cover.

She'd made a list on another piece of paper of random things to talk to him about. She wanted to paint the kitchen, use the third bedroom for the kids, and bring her Nespresso machine.

Oh, God.

He read a printed email in which Cara Marshall had gone apoplectic over Laura's apparent decision to give him the proceeds from the sale of her house.

"What is she doing?" He thought out loud. "Laura!"

There was a business card from Chase Markham, the only realtor in town, with some figures scribbled on it along the notation, "Will this be enough?"

He sat down on the couch and ran a hand through his hair. In his mind it should have been so simple because he just wanted her with him. He had been hurt, thinking that she didn't want to move in, but he hadn't considered that he was asking her to uproot her life and her business. He couldn't believe she'd been as patient as she was.

While the idea of living together was liberating for him, he realized then that his house might feel more like a cage to her. Though he hadn't shown it at all, he did respect her independence and feared that in his enthusiasm he probably stepped all over plans she hadn't yet shared with him along with things that were none of his damn business.

"Laura!" An even deeper feeling of dread came upon him as he finally looked around her darkened house. He followed a crackling noise through the kitchen and his chest tightened when the shattered glass crunched underneath his footsteps in the doorway. "Laura!"

He shoved the broken table out of the way and stormed onto the patio, picking up the fire extinguisher that had tumbled out of the grill cabinet. Small fires burned everywhere, threatening the main part of the house so he sprayed them out one by one until he came across where Watson lay whimpering under the upended grill.

As he pulled out his phone, Audi, in following her mother's instructions to check on Laura, picked her way through the door.

"Auntie?" She stepped outside and turned in circles amidst the damage shrieking at Bash, "What the hell happened here?"

He put up a finger up, and said, "Hang on." Then he dialed Chuck's number and put the phone on speaker mode, propping it up on what was left of the table.

Chuck and Drew had just finished up a wellness check

on Missy's boyfriend, Josh, when the call came through. Bash could barely keep the hysteria out of his voice when Chuck answered.

"He took her, he took her right out of her fucking house."

They heard Audi consoling Watson in the background, "Hold still buddy, we're gonna help you right now."

Bash's voice strained further as he lifted the grill, "Pull him out! Pull him out!" The grill crashed to the ground when Watson was free and Drew took the phone in a panic.

"Bash, you've got to stop and talk to us."

"How could I be so stupid? My God, there's blood and fire everywhere."

Gravel flew as Chuck spun the wheel and threw the old county truck into a U-turn.

With the exception of her mother, everyone found Laura's home welcoming. Until that night, it had always been very much an extension of her, both magical and warm. Drew noticed the shift in energy right away and shivered as they walked through cold patches of dead air in the house. She had told them once that plants tried to keep humans safe by absorbing bad energy. Even in the dark, he could see that all of Laura's plants were dead.

As he and Chuck poked their way through the house, they heard a crashing noise from Laura's bedroom. They drew their pistols and called out for their friend. Hearing no answer, they burst into the room to find Bash tearing up her bathroom for first aid supplies. They lowered their guns as he pushed past them.

"Watson's hurt. I don't know if he's gonna make it."

They followed him out back where Audi sat on the ground with Watson's head in her lap. Drew holstered his gun, took the gauze and peroxide from Bash and they got to work on the German Shepherd's wounds.

Chuck put his hands on Bash's shoulders. "Show me everything, and we'll put it together."

Forcing himself into sheriff mode calmed Bash immensely and he was better able to focus as he led Chuck around the clues on the porch.

Her tiger's eye bracelet lay in a pool of blood next to the broken rosemary planter. "I don't know if this is her blood or not." Bash picked up the bracelet and wiped it on his shirt. "God, Chuck, she could be in another dimension right now."

Audi grabbed Drew's arm. "I bet he has her in the cave."

The three men stared at her.

"There's a cave. It's over the bridge and across the river. We saw the light the day we met him."

Chuck was already dialing his phone by the time she finished her sentence. "The vehicles won't make it—not even her Jeep. We'll need horses to get back there."

When he hung up, he said, "The stables are getting ready for us."

Bash dropped the bracelet in his pocket. "How long?"

"Soon. Let's go to the station and get what we need. I'll call Rhonda to sit with Watson and Audi."

Audi bristled. "Are you new?" She and Drew were already climbing into the backseat of the cramped county truck.

Bash leaned his head against the window of the passenger seat as Chuck sped away from Laura's house.

"You need to know that this is my fault. We had a fight and, Christ, I hung up on her."

Chuck ignored his confession. "Did I ever tell you how I met Laura?"

"In high school?"

"Yeah, man, I think we were sophomores." He chuckled. "We used to have these big bonfire parties out in the desert. Old Sheriff Vance didn't really care, but he had this deputy who thought he was some kind of second coming. The county had a 'three strikes and you're out' position on troubled kids at the time."

Bash huffed. "I'm familiar with that rule—had two strikes myself."

Audi's eyes widened and her respect for Sheriff Scott elevated slightly.

"Anyway, this kid, I can't remember his name now, but he was one of *those* kids. Not a bad guy, but he always found himself in trouble for one reason or another."

Bash nodded, thinking Chuck could have been talking about him at that age.

"I had a huge crush on Mena," Chuck continued, "and that night we were sitting on top of somebody's truck drinking cheap beer and wine coolers when a fight broke out—you know how they do at those things. Wouldn't you know it, that kid finds himself taking a swing just as Deputy Dickhead shows up. Everybody knew that he was gonna go to grown-up jail if he got arrested again."

"So, Laura pulled out some of that bonfire and

jumped in the middle of the fight, shielding the boy long enough for him to get away. Then, she picked up a four pack of Bartles and Jaymes and offered one to the deputy. Do you believe that shit? And while I was getting Mena and Sarah out of there, Laura was getting shoved in the back of the deputy's car in handcuffs."

"That's my girl." Bash wished he'd known her back then. Although, he was pretty sure they would have gotten each other killed doing stupid stuff before they ever had a chance to learn what real trouble was like.

"I heard that story," Audi piped up from the back seat. "Mom said Nana whipped Auntie so bad that she couldn't go to school for days, and I heard she was grounded for a whole month."

Chuck made a grim face. "My point is that your girl has always been able to think fast, she's always been powerful, and she's never been afraid of pain."

Chapter Thirteen

Not half an hour later they were fully supplied, saddled up, and making their way to the natural bridge. Chuck caught Andrew wobbling a bit in the saddle and whispering into his horse's ear.

"When was the last time you rode a horse, man?"

Drew laughed nervously, "About fifteen years ago, but I believe Stranger and I have come to an understanding. I won't make any sudden moves and he won't throw me into a cactus. Right, boy?"

As they approached the bridge, they aimed their flashlights at the ground so as not to confuse the horses while they searched the area.

"There," Audi pointed, "see that light flickering at the base of the butte?"

"Put these on." Drew tossed them each a cross. "Apparently trolls hate them."

"This feels hypocritical," Bash complained, "don't you have to be a believer for this sort of thing to work?"

"Your girlfriend is half angel, man." Chuck reminded him.

"Well, I'm an unenthusiastic believer."

Chuck was sympathetic. "Where is Daniel anyway?" he asked, "He's useless. Don't think I don't notice he only shows up when he wants something. That's some bullshit."

"We've never crossed the bridge before," Audi warned. "I don't even know if we can."

Bash set his jaw and nudged his horse forward. "I'll go first."

Keeping their eyes on the light coming from the cave, they crossed the bridge single file without incident until they'd traveled about a quarter of a mile. Three mule deer darted across their paths, spooking Stranger a bit, so Drew loosened the reins and patted his neck.

"Easy...easy."

Bash turned in the saddle to face the others, announcing flatly, "Those deer were silver, so be on the lookout for all kinds of creatures."

They followed the bank of the dry riverbed for another mile when the horses began to get really nervous. Bash moved close and ran his fingers through Stranger's mane. It was as much an attempt to calm the horse as to calm his friend who was increasingly worried about getting thrown.

Chuck rode up beside them. "Do you hear that?"

Drew listened hard. "Water?"

"The river's been dry for years and we haven't gotten *that* much rain this summer."

The horses remained agitated, so they dismounted and walked them back to some Mesquite trees, tying them off and leaving them with plenty of treats.

"We're close now." They took the supplies and weapons and slid down some giant white rocks, moving as quickly as possible. The sound of rushing water grew louder the deeper they travelled into the riverbed. Midway across, they had to squint from the light of the moon and Drew squeezed his fingertips on the bridge of his nose as a headache came on out of the blue.

They turned off their flashlights and looked anxiously at one another as an eerie silence closed in around them. The water was still out there, somewhere; but nothing rustled in the bushes, no coyotes howled, and no insects chirped.

Drew was uneasy. "Something's watching us."

"Look at the rocks," Audi noted, "look how they shine in the moonlight, almost like crystals." She scooped some sand into her palm and sifted it through her fingers. "Feels like cashmere."

They studied their surroundings and though nothing had changed, everything was different. It was as if they had suddenly developed high-definition night vision and it was throwing them slightly off balance.

It was when their boots in the sand went from crunching to squishing that what they feared became a certainty. Water seeped out of the ground, covering their feet, and they knew they'd somehow travelled to the Other Side.

"The river's filling," Chuck cautioned, "we've got to get across...now."

They waded as fast as they could, then swam as the water reached their waists. It wasn't cold and the current was calm, but it would be over their heads in minutes. Just as it reached his chest, Bash hauled himself up the other bank and the others lifted Audi into his arms.

Their clothes dried the instant they were out of the water and Chuck was mumbling something about small favors when Bash shushed him. They could hear voices coming from the entrance to the cave, which was just overhead.

Inside the cave, Laura woke to find her hands bound and separated far enough that she couldn't rub them together. Richard used the same thing to tie her ankles and she was surprised that though it was thick, the rope had the texture of satin. Silky or not, he had the skill of an Eagle Scout and the more she struggled, the deeper the knots dug into her skin.

She closed her eyes, unable to believe that she'd been so vulnerable to his attack. Thomas didn't have to send Tromluí for them, they'd managed to become separated and ineffective all on their own.

"Hey, now." Richard wore a new costume consisting of a soft looking forest green tunic over pants made from a thicker version of the same fabric. His boots were wool, and an amulet emblazoned with the same sigil she'd seen when they fought the harpies hung from his neck on a braided gold chain. She could feel the magic pulsing from it.

Convinced that no one would come for her, she prepared herself for the worst but, eyeing the amulet, she devised a plan just in case she caught a break.

"Oh, do you like this?" He pulled it over his head and brought it to her. "This is a pass that gets me to and from the Other Side, in case you were wondering how I made it to your house. I was lonely all those years guarding a bridge that so few ever tried to cross. I suppose that means humans are smarter than they get credit for, but you're the first one to answer my riddle."

"Your riddle was easy," she mumbled, "it was easy on purpose."

"The thing you need to know about me," he knelt and showed her the mark Drew's cross left on his forearm, "is that all I want is justice."

She screamed and smoke sizzled as he pressed the amulet to her temple, burning the sigil into her skin.

Hearing Laura scream, Bash scrambled up the embankment and found himself facing Adira at the top.

"He wants her assistance, Sebastian," she latched her teeth onto his vest and pulled him up the rest of the way, "but Laura is not cooperating, so there isn't much time."

"Auntie's not cooperating?" Audi mused. "There's a shocker."

Bash stumbled as he stood up, paling from worry induced nausea.

Drew gripped his forearms in support. "She's alive," he comforted, "Bash, look at me—we know she's alive."

"This way, quickly." Adira led them to an ancient looking tree, robust with soft leaves at the top yet sparse on the bottom with dead tendrils of branches hanging low into thick roots jutting up from the earth. Bash pulled out a small machete and made to hack away at the gnarled structure, but she nipped at his hand.

Drew stepped forward and, on a whim, pushed his fingers through. The branches were silky to his touch and he brushed them back as if they were a curtain.

"Pretty," Audi cooed.

"Let's go." Bash pushed through into a tunnel lined

with wildflowers growing up the walls, twisting themselves around knots of cacti hanging down from the top. He gestured for his friends to protect their heads and they travelled single file until the Bobs popped through the flowers in the wall, directing them to follow.

In smaller voices that they had not heard before, both Bobs spoke as one in their minds.

"Come."

"Come."

Chuck sighed, "Nothing is ever gonna be weird to me after this night, man."

"You didn't drag me here because you got a boo boo." Laura tried to sit up. "Why did you hurt those kids? You didn't have to kill that boy."

"That's your fault," Richard shrugged his shoulders, "I couldn't get your attention."

"Fuck you." She spat at him.

He kicked her over. "You'd better behave yourself or I won't tell you my secret."

She let her head rest on the floor of the cave and considered her situation. But for the smooth ground, the cave itself was like the inside of a geode, lit by the moonlight as it bounced off the crystals. It must have been the reflection of the sun in the cave they had seen the day they first met him by the bridge.

"You like my home, too?" He ran his hands along the walls, demonstrating that though they were lined with crystals, they were not jagged. "This whole butte is hollow. It's one big crystal cave."

She tried sitting up again. "Keep that to yourself or

you'll have every collector in the world digging it up."

"It wouldn't be the first time I've had to move." He pulled her upright by the hair and leaned her against the wall. "We all lived together once when there was no Other Side. Humans, angels, gods, and creatures of all kinds walked around the earth like we owned the place." He smoothed her dress over her knees and put his face close to hers, yelling, "Because we did!"

"But when your god got angry, the angels forced all the old ones over to the Other Side. They said they were protecting us from the flood." He ignored her glare and paced in front of her. "Ask your father—he was there."

"Don't get me wrong, it's nice here and I can appreciate being saved from the 'great drowning'." He rolled his eyes. "It's just that we don't all get along and some of us would like to move out."

"Humans don't get along either."

He stooped to pick up a sprig of rosemary that had gotten stuck in her dress. "I would like to have the choice."

"You can obviously come and go as you please."

"We can't spend too much time on your Side, and we certainly don't travel far from a gate because the veil is too unpredictable. A very clever trap, by the way." He dropped the rosemary into her lap. "It could thicken at any time and we would be stuck, but I've recently learned that there's a plan to move the portals around."

"Do you really think that humans will just let you be?"

"Their race is weak with a crumbling society."

It was disturbing that he didn't include her when he spoke of the human race. "I still don't understand what you want from me."

"If enough of us come across and begin to build our lives, there will be no more need for portals and the world could go back to the way it was."

She'd been waiting patiently and, finally, he leaned close to her again. On that Side of the veil, his hair wasn't gray, but a shimmering, soft silver. She raised her bound wrists and grabbed a handful of it, pulling his head to the ground.

He hit hard but reached up and pressed his thumb deep into the top of her hand. Ignoring the pain, she whispered a hex in his ear. As he writhed away from her, she sealed the hex by scratching the rosemary sprig across his face.

Richard struggled clumsily to his feet and kicked her over again. "Bitch!" He gathered a much longer piece of satin rope that hung from a small tree just inside the cave, threaded it through the knot between her wrists and threw it over a large crystal that jutted from the wall. She screamed again as he jerked on the rope, hauling her to her feet with her arms overhead.

He tied off the rope and grabbed her chin. "Your magic doesn't work here."

Angry tears seeped from the corners of her eyes, streaking dirt down her cheeks. "Then why don't you light us a fire? I'm cold."

"I love that you can lie so easily." He wiped the sweat from her temples with the back of his hand. "Believe it or not, I still don't want to hurt you. I'm giving you the chance to walk away. Back off, let nature take its course and promise to use your power when we need you to help us reclaim what is ours."

She shook her head furiously.

"Your kind locked me up over here and you owe

me justice. One way or another, I will return to your Side. All you have to do is make a choice. Are you going to do the right thing or not?"

She lifted her knees and kicked at him. "You're a bully and a prick and I don't want you on my Side."

Chapter Fourteen

Bash and the others emerged from the tunnel right outside of Richard's cave. At the sight of Laura tied up and fighting, Audi threw her rocks in the air and waved her arms, hurling them as hard as she could into the troll's torso. Richard rushed for her, but she ducked away and Bash tackled him to the ground.

She and Drew set about cutting through Laura's ropes with the machete.

Richard jerked Bash up, threw him against the wall and punched him in the stomach, then Bash grabbed Richard's shoulders and kneed him in the groin, landing an upper cut to his jaw as he doubled over.

Bash slipped into a blind rage and, as Richard fell backward onto the ground, pounced on top of him, punching him the face over and over until he heard Chuck rack the slide on his pistol.

The troll gaped at Chuck through his swollen eyes. "You brought iron into this place?"

"You betcha," Drew said, aiming a shotgun just inches from his face.

Richard tried to shrink away but Bash held him on the ground as Chuck threatened, "We will riddle this place with so much buckshot you'll never find it all. This cave will wither into nothingness if you ever come for my people again."

"Guys, get back." Audi held Laura up with an arm around her waist.

The men dove out of the way as Audi flicked a zippo and Laura threw a stream of fire directly into Richard's center of mass.

Adira roared from outside the cave. "You cannot kill him here but, if you leave now, you can get away with your own lives."

Laura slumped against Bash and they all followed Adira, dropping their crosses in a line along the cave's entryway as they left.

"The troll is hated on this Side, but your safety is not guaranteed."

They raced through the tree tunnel, exiting on the bank of the river. Laura's knees buckled at the sight of it and Bash lifted her panicked face in his hands. "Come on, baby, we've got to swim." He took her arm and led her into the water.

"We'll get some rope to help you." Chuck dove in with Audi and they sped across.

Drew waded in and took Laura's other arm. "Just keep your eyes forward."

Crossing was painful and slow, and they could see creatures of all kinds lining up along the banks and goblins watching them from the bushes. Eventually, Audi swam out with rope that they tied around Laura's waist. Bash held on while Chuck reeled them in and Drew hurried Audi back to the shore.

As they mounted their horses, the Bobs approached, flanked by three enormous gray wolves. When Bash had Laura secured in front of him, the wolves sprinted ahead while the Bobs pushed at his feet in the stirrups.

"Follow."

"Follow."

"Fast."

"Fast."

Bash dug into the flanks of his horse. "Hyah!"

Audi and Chuck raced behind him but Stranger hesitated, looking back at Drew. "It's okay, I trust you." Drew held tight as Stranger lit out after the others.

The wolves chased alongside them, howling and snapping to keep the goblins away until they crossed the bridge.

Back at Laura's house, Bash dismounted, and she fell into his arms. Rhonda led them through the darkness, though it glowed warmly because she had lit every candle she could find. Watson laid on a blanket next to the couch and nuzzled Laura's knees when Bash rested her on the cushions.

Chuck called for the stable manager. "If she's still awake, I'll get the horses back and find us some food."

"I'm guessing she is." According to the clock on Drew's phone, they'd been gone just under an hour. He knew that wasn't right but was not surprised that time passed more slowly on the Other Side. He flipped through his list of contacts and started making calls of his own.

When Chuck left, Drew stepped back into the

house, trying unsuccessfully to avoid crunching through the broken glass, and announced, "Adam's on his way with a generator, Laura, and we'll have your power back on soon." He took a water bottle from the refrigerator, then ducked back outside to wait.

The water was already tepid, so he made a mental note that everything else in the fridge would have to be tossed. Between them they could restore the house in a few days, but he doubted that the damage done to Laura could ever be repaired.

Audi and Rhonda set about checking Laura for injuries, focusing on the blood that still oozed from the knife wound across her palm. "We need Noah for this."

She pushed them away and stood up, wrapping her arms around herself. "I didn't think you would come for me."

"Of course we would, Auntie."

Laura looked at Bash and sobbed. "I...I thought you didn't know what happened."

He took her into his arms. "I came over to apologize and you were gone."

"But how..."

"Shhh, we don't have to talk about that now."

She pulled away from him, her eyes flashing angry in the candlelight. "Never, *ever* shush me again." Then she turned to Audi, "I want to take a bath."

"On it!" Audi grabbed two candles and led her to the bathroom.

Bash hit the wall lightly with his fist and stormed outside where he ran into Drew and Adam setting up lanterns around the porch. He helped them wrestle a generator off the trailer behind Adam's truck, noting that he and Drew apparently had the much lighter part of the load.

"No, no buddy there's too much glass." Watson had hobbled out to check on them, and when Bash tried to stop him, the dog stood stubbornly in the doorway.

Watson weighed well over one hundred pounds, and the others struggled to believe it when Adam scooped him up and brought him to a safe space on the porch.

"He's just worried and he wants to be with you guys."

Bash followed a green light blinking under the table and plucked Laura's phone from a mess of broken tiles. It was still showing the notification for his voicemail message. He snatched a brick that had come loose from the wall, turned away from them and threw it as hard as he could across the back yard.

Rhonda put her arms around him and rested her mop of long gray curls just below his chin. "Don't take this all on yourself, sweetie. She doesn't communicate any better than you do. The two of you will rush in anywhere to fight monsters but you're deathly afraid to talk about your feelings. It boggles the mind."

Bash relaxed into Rhonda's embrace, missing his mother for the first time in months. "I'm afraid Laura fell for the biggest asshole in town."

Adam paused his work, "In Chuparosa that would be quite an accomplishment, so don't go flattering yourself." He fed the cord through the panel at the top of the meter and shook his head at Drew. "Are you seeing this? Everything is fried."

Drew unscrewed the cap on top of the generator and poured in diesel fuel from a gas can, "You're thinking you should have been here, but I don't know,

Bash," he kicked the mutilated panel cover out of their workspace, "look at that. He might have killed you first and who knows what would be happening to her right now."

They finished connecting the wires, turned on the generator and then the breaker. When the power pulsed on, Rhonda left them to secure the rest of the house.

"Thanks guys." Bash said, and then exchanged glances with Drew. Watson was heavy, and the generator weighed a few hundred pounds. "Do you, uh, want to come inside, Adam?"

Adam shook his head, aware he'd been found out, but still a bit hesitant to show his full hand.

"You know she has to be the one to invite me in, and I'm all dirty anyway." With one arm he lifted the grill off the ground and set it upright.

Bash balled his fists at his sides. They'd speculated about Adam but were unsure until just then. There was only one monster that truly frightened Sebastian Scott. It didn't just scare him, it kept him awake sometimes just knowing that vampires existed. In fact, the thought of vampires would stop him in his tracks if it occurred to him in the middle of the day.

Adam could smell the fear circulating on the porch and took a step back to accommodate the other two men.

After everything he'd been through that night, Bash could not find his words, so Drew began the interrogation. "When were you going to tell us?"

"Well, I'm not particularly proud of it and, further, it's not the kind of thing I go around announcing to everyone I meet. The more people who know, the more dangerous it is for me. You two are the first real friends

I made since coming to Chuparosa, but you are new friends and I had to be careful."

"Cara, too?" Drew asked.

"Does Laura know?" Bash finally blurted.

"Laura does not know. And yes, Cara is..." he paused, "a new development for me."

"Christ." Bash doubled over and put his hands on his knees.

"Sebastian, please look at me," Adam moved closer to them and held out his hands, "you have to understand that I will never hurt you or your people."

"I can't." Bash straightened and shook his head. "I just can't do this right now." He stumbled through the glass and left them on the porch.

They were quiet while Drew tried to figure out how to proceed with the conversation but, eventually Adam looked around and changed the subject completely.

"The spirits in this house are very uneasy."

"Spirits?" Drew asked.

"All homes have spirits and even if Laura doesn't know them, she somehow takes good care of them because they love her. The energy here must have been phenomenal until tonight because they are devastated by what's happened here."

"You could see spirits the other night at the bar, couldn't you?"

Adam nodded and decided to fully out himself, biting into his finger and allowing a few drops of blood to drip into Watson's mouth. The dog whimpered a few more times, then jumped up and turned in confused circles. Adam bent and nuzzled his neck. "That's a good boy."

He ignored Drew's look of astonishment and

continued his assessment of the house. "Laura's wards are shattered and this place is vulnerable. I know my confession must feel like piling on to you tonight but, if you guys can stand it, I'll stay out here and keep watch until dawn."

"You've been a good friend to us, Adam, and we have no reason not to trust you. Honestly, you could have told me you are Adam from the book of Genesis, and it wouldn't surprise me at this point."

A sudden, worried look crossed Drew's face so Adam held up his hands. "Nope, just Adam from Bisbee."

Drew scratched the back of his head. "A vampire living in Arizona? Do you have no self-preservation instincts at all?"

"There are vampires everywhere."

Drew sighed. "That won't comfort Bash."

Adam shrugged. "He already knows, or he wouldn't be so scared. I'm guessing there's one hell of a story there, but we may never find out how he managed to live to tell it—trauma being what it is and all."

Drew waved his hand dismissively and piled shards of the giant planter along the edge of the porch. "Nah, it just hasn't come up until now. We're experts at trauma from way back."

"Well, then," Adam plucked the rosemary bush from the ground and shook the glass out of the roots. "I'm afraid I'll fit in nicely."

"It's me." Bash knocked softly on the bathroom door.

Rhonda poked her head out. "Go on in, sweetie, I'm taking Audi home with me and tomorrow we'll bring back supplies."

Though the power was somewhat restored, the bathroom was lit only with candles. The air was thick with steam and smelled of eucalyptus. Herbs and flowers floated around her on top of the water and Laura rested her head on her knees. Bash lowered himself to the floor next to the tub and took the sponge from her hand, squeezing the steaming water across her back.

"I thought I lost you tonight, and I couldn't fucking breathe. Baby, I'm so—"

"It's on both of us," she interrupted. "When you consider all of the shit we've been through together, the fact that we made each other feel 'less than' is unacceptable, Bash. We're always second guessing ourselves in the name of being together and its absurd." She took his hand. "You think that I don't need you, but you're wrong. I need you so much, and it scares me to death because I know what you've already taken on to be with me."

"Laura, I was dying inside," his voice broke, and he cleared his throat to continue, "I don't know how much of me was already gone but I thought coming to Chuparosa was the end. I thought I was just gonna live the rest of my days hiding out in this small town. Hell, I figured I'd be shot to death by a wife beater or blown up in a meth lab by now."

He laid his head on her shoulder. "But it was the beginning of everything. You, my friends, my job, and this damn town are everything to me. My life finally means something," he laughed, "which is why I expect it to end any day now. I've been hanging on so tight that I just couldn't see what you needed from me."

"Sebastian, you are my hero and in ways that have nothing to do with the fact that you literally rode in on a horse and rescued me tonight." She let go of his hand and laid back in the tub, letting the warm water cover her body. "Don't think I don't know that's always been a fantasy of yours."

He laughed again but his eyes reddened and he wiped at the tears with the back of his hand before they could fall. "I appreciate you indulging me, but just this once, okay? And from now on, I don't care if we're doing battle in Hell itself, if we've got a problem, we drop everything and talk about it until we're good."

She sat up and kissed his cheek, his chin, and then his lips. "The world can burn down around us."

In the living room, Drew flopped on the couch and put his arms behind his head. He thought for a while about ways he might build a bridge between Adam and Bash. Then he wondered if Bash would ever be able to forgive himself for his fight with Laura, though everyone knew the evening's main events were not his fault.

To be Laura's man was difficult—deadly even, and Drew respected the hell out of the two of them for making it work at all. In spite of their problems, they loved each other fiercely and with devotion like he'd never seen before.

His thoughts then travelled, as always, to Sarah. He doubted that she knew anything about what they had been through that night, but he hoped she knew how much they missed her. How much *he* missed her. If he got his wish, he would be accepting the same fate as his friend and he, like Bash, wanted nothing more in the world.

Chapter Fifteen

Before she'd left the valley, Sarah made arrangements to meet Brian at a small farmer's market just off campus. He was pacing in front of the fry bread stall, checking the time on his phone, when he finally saw her rushing toward him.

"Hey!" He gave her a hug and a devious look, "Guess who I met today?"

They started down the aisle. "I can't imagine."

"Becky Scott." He crossed his arms, pleased with himself over her stunned silence. "Yep. She's a grad student, studying cryptography and she plans to work on police investigations."

"Well, Bash thinks he's Magnum, P.I., so..."

"Who?"

She pursed her lips. "Never mind. My point is that crime fighting is in her blood. I had no idea she was up here."

"You would know these things if you ever talked to Mom."

For the most part, she could appreciate his

generation's frankness but, in her fragile state, chose to ignore his critique of her life choices and proceeded with her own bit of gossip. "You'll never guess what I've been up to."

"You obviously haven't become an emotional eater." Thomas said, approaching them with plates of fry bread. "Have a taco, darling, you're wasting away, and we have work to do."

His inference was irritating, but the crispy dough covered with beans and cheese was too much for her to resist so she snatched it from him with a glare.

Electricity flowed through Brian's fingers but there were far too many people at the market for him to start something and Thomas knew it.

"Make sure you clean your plate, boy," he demanded.

"You killed my husband." Sarah seethed.

"Oh, please." He held up his thumb and pointer finger. "You were this close to running off to join the cult of Andrew Clarke, were you not? Aren't you still? Gasp!" He clutched at imaginary pearls around his neck. "Or are you content to keep breaking his heart? How long do you think he'll wait for you?"

Thomas's affinity for poking at emotional wounds was extraordinary and it enraged her how frequently he hit the nail on the head with his observations. She had nothing to say except, "Rueben didn't have to die."

He smirked at her. "Rueben's demise was based entirely on decisions he made throughout his life, just like yours will be."

"Tell that to Audi." Brian spat.

"Don't pretend to be mad, Sarah—not after what you did for me at Vista Pines today."

Remembering Rebecca's phone conversation, Brian dropped his fry bread in a nearby trash bin and bent his knees to be at eye level with Sarah. "Auntie, why were you at Vista Pines?"

"That's where your great grandma Fiona lives." She thumbed at Thomas. "And Fiona tried to poison him earlier."

Brian began to get worried. "Becky has an interview with someone in Vista Pines at 4 p.m."

"You know, Sarah," Thomas walked around her, looking her up and down with fresh curiosity. "I never gave you much thought. You've really never been more to me than 'the spare', but when I think about it now, I probably should have approached you first. You're definitely the spoiled youngest child and you've got extraordinary power stored up inside."

Sarah laughed bitterly. "My mother didn't spoil me."

"The boy alluded to it a few minutes ago, but he has more respect for your feelings than I do, so I'll just run with it now. You were spoiled by your sister. Laura shielded you from your mother's worst and now you won't even talk to her."

Thomas paused as they passed a crystal vendor's table. "Aren't there supposed to be vegetables at a farmer's market?"

An assortment of citrine piled high on a velvet table runner caught Sarah's attention and she selected a piece to admire. The vendor was busy with another customer and when she returned the stone to the pile, Thomas glowered over the table. Seconds later, all of the citrine shattered into loose crumbs. She grabbed his arm and dragged him away.

"Stop that—it is obnoxious and beneath you."

He shrugged. "It's not really beneath me."

Brian's phone rang and he'd barely said, "Hello" when a hysterical Audi began to tell him about her last twenty-four hours. "Wait, what? Slow down."

She told him of Richard, what happened to Watson, their trip to the Other Side, and how Sheriff Scott fought the troll for Laura.

Thomas cracked his knuckles, and a pile of aventurine was reduced to dust. Turning to Brian he said, "I suppose we will have to admit that the cowboy *does* have his uses." He steepled his fingers and jibed, "Too bad his daughter is walking into a trap."

Sarah led them farther away from the crystal table and took the phone. "Audra, honey it's me."

"Mom! Everyone is so worried about you."

She calmed her daughter for a few minutes and then noted that the time was 3 p.m. "Audi, we have one more thing to do and then I'm coming home."

Thomas curled his lip as Sarah handed Brian his phone. "Even now Laura wouldn't trouble you with what happened to her because her concern is for *you*."

"I didn't know he was a troll."

"But you knew he was dangerous, and you still ran away. She's a pain in my ass but I've always respected your sister. I realize now though, that you're the one I can actually relate to."

Two stalls down, Daniel stood in front of a local honey display and took a bite of his own fry bread.

"That is the last thing I wanted to hear."

* * *

It was September first and inasmuch as Arizona has a fall season, Laura had started decorating for it before their battle with the harpies. She was sick of the sweltering summer heat and, though it was all in her head, dragging out the bins of gnomes and pumpkins convinced her of a slight chill in the air.

She truly loved Halloween but as witch she also felt obliged to keep her neighbors on their toes by drawing attention to the fact with a few not so subtle reminders. Having been the subject of gossip and speculation since she was a teenager, it gave her no small amount of joy to hang a pentacle wreath and draw symbols in chalk on her front door every year.

Drew Clarke was the only one who ever dared to ask about the symbols. He laughed until his sides hurt when she confessed that they were meaningless. She would never invite trouble by drawing real magic on her door—not magic that people could see, anyway. Drew agreed that the local busybodies didn't need to know that and promised to take her secret to his grave.

Adding to Laura's personal stash of decorations, Sonia Trainer gave her three pumpkins from an early batch in her garden. Laura had already drawn out the faces for them, but they'd been smashed across the back porch with everything else during Richard's attack.

"Gross." Audi crouched to scoop it up with a spatula, but Watson licked off the orange goo before she could toss it in a trash bag.

Laura was unable to face the damage to her herb garden out back and busied herself with clearing out the warm refrigerator and the dead plants inside.

Drew sat at her kitchen table looking back and forth from his laptop to a pile of open books and jumped up to help as she climbed a step ladder to pull the plants from atop her cabinets. She was covered in cuts and bruises and moving slowly. He worried that she was hurt much worse than she let on, but she refused to let them take her to the hospital, so he kept the conversation to the tasks at hand.

"How long will it take to repair your wards?"

She handed him a blackened porthos and sighed. "I was pregnant with Brian when I bought this house. It's a cumulative process."

"Oh, Laura..."

"It's a good thing I'm moving out," she winked at Bash as he hopped over the mangled doorstep, "but I have a better understanding of what we're dealing with now, so I won't be taking any chances with his house."

"Our house," Bash corrected.

Drew twisted the shield bracelet around his wrist, puzzling over how twenty-one years of protective magic could be obliterated in one night. What exactly *were* they dealing with?

Bash followed Drew outside and stood by while he inspected the generator. "What do you make of that mark on her temple?"

"It's the sigil from his amulet," Drew said, "and it matches the ones we saw in the desert the night we fought the harpies, but I can't find it anywhere in the research."

Bash kicked at a piece of pumpkin and gritted his teeth. "He branded her with it."

Audi tied up a bag of porch debris and announced, "Head's up," as Daniel approached from the south side of the house.

Laura sauntered past him, dumping an armload of

dead houseplants into the firepit. "Long time, no see. How's *your* day going?"

He ignored her sarcasm. "We have to talk about your sister."

"She went to Flagstaff for a break. Did you forget that your brother murdered her husband?"

Daniel folded his arms across his chest. "She's with Thomas and your grandmother right now."

Drew stepped forward. "I don't believe you."

"Sarah is on a passage from pain, but she is not grieving in the traditional sense. She is practicing dangerous magic."

"Speaking of dangerous magic," Bash grumped, "we could have used a hand last night."

"I cannot go to the Other Side," Daniel pushed Laura's hair behind her ear, revealing the mark left by the troll. "I was unsure if you could until now. It's fortunate any of you survived."

He traced the mark on her temple until she pushed away from him. "It burns."

"I'm not surprised. This is some of the first magic ever written."

"That's why I couldn't find it," Drew threw his head back. "it's not a symbol, it's a language."

Daniel nodded, "If said correctly, this spell can shift space, which explains what's happening in other parts of the world."

"I don't think Thomas gave it to the troll," Laura offered. "They have very different agendas."

In a low voice Daniel said, "Sarah is part of his agenda now and she needs to be stopped."

Laura moved in front of him and matched his tone, "Sarah needs to be helped, not hunted."

Bash gently pulled her close to him. "Leave Sarah alone and let us handle anything that comes up. That's what you do best right?"

"I'm tired of this," Drew lashed out, "all you do is manipulate and threaten us."

"I am protecting—"

"Who do you protect?" Drew pointed at himself and to Bash. "Not us," then, he pointed at Laura, "not even your own kind. You make all these demands but you're never there when we need you. You always seem to be watching, but where have you been? How long have you been there?"

"How far away were you when Brona was torturing her daughters for all those years? Were you watching Bash when he was fighting for his child from a battlefield thousands of miles away from her? Were you watching me?" He pulled off his t-shirt and turned to show Daniel the scars on his back. "Your people did these things to us—your most devoted servants. But Sarah is the one you're going after?"

"Those aren't my people, Andrew. Their time will come, but so will yours."

Drew lunged for Daniel, but Bash held him back and Laura stepped between them, extending her arms defensively between them all. She flicked her fingernails, pulling fire into one of her palms. After her experience with Richard, she would never again be caught without the ability to defend herself and she had no problem testing her latest phosphorescent mixture on an angel.

"Don't you touch him."

Daniel spoke slowly, "I'm not going to hurt him, and I won't be robbing him of those who love him so much they would do battle with an angel of God on his behalf."

Drew spat on the ground. "You brought us together. For all our lives, you made sure we were fucked up enough to fight in your war, and now you're worried that we might be a little too fucked up? Well, that's too bad. I get that we're expendable to you, but we're also done with you."

Daniel shook his head. "Whether we work together or not, your cause is my cause. You have got to understand that I don't want to be your enemy. But I'm not in charge of this."

Bash held tight against Drew's struggling. "You're just a drone like us and we won't take orders from you. This is our team, not yours. We know what needs to happen and we can do it without you—it won't be that much different anyway."

The unexpected truth in Sebastian's words pierced like a nail in Daniel's heart. In his arrogance he'd not expected them to be willing to do the job on their own. He thought that since they had no choice but to believe, they would follow him without question. He never considered that one of the effects of their suffering would be a willingness to abandon any hope they had of redemption, simply accepting whatever fate had in store for them. That they weren't quitting but were doing right just for the sake of it, moved him like no other experience with human beings ever had.

"You're right Sebastian, and I want to help you."

Laura pulled the stone Daniel gave her from around her neck and let it drop on the ground, "But you have your orders."

"It's so unfair." Bash said under his breath.

"You can't see anything that matters." Though his body was still taut with emotion, Drew relaxed enough that Bash let him go. "We know way more about Thomas than we do about you. He's psychotic, but at least his story is sympathetic."

Daniel raised his hands, "What am I supposed to do?"

"It's pretty simple." Bash rubbed his forehead. Their emotions were all over the place and they were tired, hungry, scared, and sore. Looking across the yard, he was grateful to see that Watson kept Audi at a safe distance and he hoped that Thomas was somehow doing the same for Sarah up north.

"Right now, we have no reason to trust you. We've spent our whole lives paying our dues, so if you want to be part of our team, you'll have to pay yours."

"If your boss gets pissed, we'll see if we can get you a deluxe suite in Hell," Laura snarked. "Nowhere near ours, of course."

Chapter Sixteen

At 3:45, Sarah and Brian crept through the woods near Fiona's trailer. A young woman Sarah had seen the day before loaded boxes into a white van parked outside and another one was chopping wood into small logs. Sarah could sense the spell Fiona had on them and knew she was out of her depth in that regard. She would have to use caution and find out what else the old woman was capable of.

Brian held her back as she advanced toward the trailer, "They'll see us."

Sarah touched the crystal at her waist and grabbed his hand. "I'm not sure if this will work on both of us at the same time, but we'll find out soon enough."

One of the girls stepped over the puddle at the foot of the steps and walked right past them.

Brian gaped at his aunt. "You have to show me how to do that."

A small car with a rideshare logo on the windshield pulled up and Becky Scott jumped out of the back seat. Sarah recognized Bash in her with one look at the girl's big brown eyes.

Becky leaned into the driver's window. "Can you wait for me?"

The driver must have declined because as he sped away, she flipped him off and hollered, "Thanks for nothing, asshole!" Thus, providing further confirmation that she was, indeed, Sebastian's daughter.

Fiona fake-hobbled to the door to greet her guest, musing bitterly that soon infirmity would no longer be just a part for her to play. Since the first witch's knock, her health was fading faster than ever and her failure to ensnare Thomas complicated the rest of plans. As soon as she had Rebecca's *cooperation,* they would travel to Chuparosa. She would most certainly be walking into a trap, but she only needed a small window of time to make her scheme come together.

Becky's guard was already up, given the neighborhood, and she realized her mistake right away from a quick glance around the little trailer. There was no doubt she'd stumbled into a witch's lair, though not the kind of witch she was familiar with.

Her father talked at length about the beautiful plants and fragrant herbs in Laura's tiny house, but Becky had been bowled over by the scent of mold and decay in Fiona's home. There was no beauty amongst the jars of dead things that lined the shelves.

Becky wondered if all witches shared some genes, because Fiona reminded her of Laura, at least in appearance. They'd only met once, but Laura was genuine and kind to her and Becky liked the smile in her father's eyes when Laura took his hand in hers. He bragged that she could weave protection into anything, but Becky knew in her bones that Fiona's intention was the opposite of keeping her safe.

She recoiled when the old woman offered her a cup of tea. "No, thank you. In fact, I think there's been a mistake and I'm going to go."

As she opened the door to leave, Fiona whispered an incantation summoning Tromluí, who whipped up the dust and pine needles while soaring past Sarah and Brian and into Becky's face.

Tromluí had become strong during its travels within the minds of the family and its power was no longer confined to the randomness of their sleeping thoughts.

In seconds it had parceled out the young woman's greatest fears and she found herself behind the iron bars of a cage with no door. A tidal wave of nausea doubled her over as claustrophobia took control of her senses. In her panic, she struggled for breath and, grabbing for the bars, she cried, "Let me out!"

In Becky's waking dream, her grandmother stood next to the cage repeating over and over, "I told you not to go...stay away from him...Lord knows it's for your own good."

Snarls and growls echoed through the darkness and she spun around to see a ferocious black mutt of a dog racing toward the cage. Her vision dotted as it threw itself at her, barking wildly and chomping at the bars. Crouching in the corner of the cage, she put her hands over her ears and screamed over and over for help, hoping she would lose her mind before the dog could get to her.

Then she remembered to find the *thing*. Too impatient for the 54321 method, she'd had some success during panic attacks in the past by redirecting her focus on one thing she could touch. She ran her trembling fingers along a jagged scar that stretched across her forearm from when she'd been attacked by a similar dog as a young teenager.

Having found her focus, her breathing slowed, and she could hear her father's voice in the distance. As it had been throughout her life, she was unable to see him, but she knew that he was there, fighting for her.

He was there for real after the incident with the dog. He'd flown across the country only to have her grandmother call the police on him. As a professional courtesy, they did not arrest him after he punched her uncle for trying to keep him out of the hospital.

Though her heart pounded loudly in her chest, she squeezed her eyes tightly and her breath continued to slow even as the top of the cage lowered and the walls moved in, forcing her further into the corner. When the cage had her pressed onto her knees, she touched the scar again and found her strength.

Her eyes flew open, and she lunged at the bars only she could see over and over until she hurled herself into Brian, who had kicked in the door of the trailer just as she broke free of her nightmare's cage.

The two young people fell out of the door past Sarah, and as they sank into the puddle, Tromluí wrapped Brian in a thin mist of mud and pinecone bits. His body twisted helplessly under the force of it until it flew away into the trees.

Sarah pushed past Fiona at the top of the steps and pulled her attention away from Becky, who was only just getting to her feet. "What did that crazy bitch do to me?"

Brian offered his arm to steady her. "You probably don't want to know."

She recognized him and recoiled. "What are *you* doing here?"

Fiona didn't know which of her granddaughters stood in front of her, but she recognized bits of Brona in Sarah's features and smiled. "I didn't think I would get to meet you so soon."

"What have you done to those girls?" Through all the commotion, Fiona's assistants continued loading up the van outside.

Fiona leaned on the kitchen counter and tried to look wounded. "I made a deal with your father, but he backed out on me, so we were gettin' ready to visit you."

"Let them go."

Fiona's back spasmed and her knees buckled. "I don't have time for this."

She gathered her strength and attempted to leave from the side door, but Sarah raised a hand and the tattered couch flew away from the wall, pushing Fiona against a low bookshelf. It was an unnecessary show of magic, but the gesture was as much a flex of her own power as a test to see what she was up against.

"I said let them go."

Fiona dragged her finger slowly along the shelf, making a face at the line in the dust. *So, Thomas wasn't lying about their powers.* "Rule number one, girl: never show off what you can do."

An oil lamp burned at the end of the shelf and as her finger reached it, Fiona stepped a foot up to the couch and casually knocked the lamp to the floor. The small explosion gave her enough time to heave herself over the furniture and out the side door while Sarah spun around looking for something to put out the flames.

"Brian!" He took the front steps in one hop and made a fist, pulling the fire into the center of the room before it could get out of control.

Something then flew into his peripheral vision and he ducked away from a huge yellow wasp that emerged from the flames as Tromluí's waking dream came for him. Again, he waved his arms to shoo it away, but several more flew at him from all corners of the trailer. He knelt and covered his head with his hands, only to find nests of scorpions crawling up through the cracks in the floor.

"Brian, get back!" Sarah pulled him away from the fire and tried to drag him out the door, but the wasps dove at them in his dream and he shoved her away to keep her safe. His t-shirt caught fire as he dreamed the scorpions pinched at him, so Sarah threw her arms around him, snuffing out the flames and knocking him against the bookshelf. His head hit the wood, waking him up in time to see her and Becky lifting the corners of an area rug.

He crawled in circles on his knees until he was satisfied that the insects were gone and then, once again, gathered most of the fire in the center of the room so the women could smother it with the rug.

They stumbled out to where the van had been and Sarah stomped her foot. "Dammit! We have to follow her!"

After they wrestled Brian into the back seat of the Cherokee, Sarah tossed Becky a first aid kit from the center console and started the engine.

He squirmed and complained as Becky ripped his t-shirt away from the burns on his chest. "Ow!"

"It's not that bad, but you don't want this to stick to you."

"Becky, where can we drop you off? We have to get back to Chuparosa as soon as we can."

She gaped at Sarah. "Are you kidding?" Tearing open a gauze pad, she announced, "After all this, I'm coming with you."

Sarah sighed. "Well, you better call your dad now or he's going to kill me later."

Becky pulled out her phone and pressed his number. "Hi Dad...yeah listen, is Laura with you? Okay good, put me on speaker. I'm with Brian and Sarah and...yes, yes, I'm alright, but I'm gonna need you to sit down and listen to me." She propped her phone between the seats and emptied the first aid kit.

"Ow!" Brian yelped again as she smeared burn cream across his chest.

"Calm down you big baby. I've burned myself worse with candle wax."

Laura leaned over the phone. "Brian? How did you get burned?"

"There were scorpions, Mom. I couldn't focus."

"What?"

"Just listen to Becky. Ow! God, it's a good thing you're not in the nursing program."

Bash slammed his fist into the back of Laura's couch. "What the hell happened?"

"I answered an ad to work for this crazy woman..."

Sarah shifted into reverse and added, "It was Fiona."

"Whoever she is," Becky continued, "she tried to put a spell on me or something and these two showed up out of the blue." She thumped on Brian's shoulder, "Were you stalking me, creep?"

Brian let his head fall onto the seat back. "Are you serious?"

"Becky!" Bash yelled.

"Right—but then she tried to burn the place down and I'm so sorry, but she got away from us.

"Jesus. Honey, it's okay."

"No Dad, I'm trying to tell you it's not okay." Becky punched the air in frustration, "She's coming to Chuparosa and bringing this whole shit show with her."

Laura was furious. "Sarah, you couldn't even send us a fucking text?"

Sarah twisted to look behind her and merged onto the interstate. "What were you going to do, Laura? Can you teleport now?"

Drew swiped the phone from Bash and took it off speaker mode. "Hello, Becky, my name is Andrew Clarke. I'm a good friend of the family."

"The preacher?"

"Yes. Tell me everything you remember, and go slow, okay? Can you start from the beginning?"

When Becky finished her story, Drew asked her to hand the phone to Sarah.

"Before you yell at me, too," she snapped at him, "things got out of hand very fast."

"Were you working with Thomas?" he asked coldly.

His tone of voice startled her and she stammered, "I...I was...against Fiona."

"Dammit, Sarah, Daniel wants to kill you."

Chapter Seventeen

One of the college girls parked the van near the train tracks and the other one sat glassy eyed and gazing into the distance from the back seat. They both jumped when Fiona started barking orders.

"Take that basket and start setting up inside. You can leave everything else for now." Their dead, disinterested looks were beginning to irritate Fiona. The smallest coven, if the women were willing and even somewhat adept would have been better than what she had to work with. She was running low on tannis root to keep them in line but, even so, none of that would matter once the healing spell was cast and her family was working for her.

Fresh spasms ripped through her back and she slammed the van door closed, leaning against it until they passed. She feared she lacked the energy to instruct the girls on every single detail, but it would have to be done. She hadn't noticed anyone in the area as they pulled in—it was an abandoned train station after all— but decided as an afterthought to throw a half-hearted hex on the van, just in case. If Thomas was right about the energy portal, she would soon be strong enough to deal with whatever came their way, including her granddaughters.

A boarded-up station house sat between two hills grown up with weeds, cacti, and brush. Trains ran daily along the new tracks that were closer to the main road, but they didn't stop at the tiny station anymore. A few boxcars sat abandoned on the old tracks and their doors were outlined with several unfamiliar sigils. Fiona approached the car that shone brightest but didn't have the strength to pull herself up the ladder.

Her curiosity would have to wait—she'd have the girls lift her up there when the spell was ready. Thomas was right, the boxcar was vibrating with energy, so much so that the sigils on the door seemed to dance across the structure. She brushed her fingertips against one of them and then yanked her hand away, swearing at the burn it left behind.

Inside the station, she prepared the hummingbird feeder she brought with her, then tore down a rotted wooden sign to hang the feeder from its hook. Outside, one of the girls emptied salt from a large canister, making a circle around the building. The spell would have to be done in the boxcar, but the circle would protect her while she was setting up in case Sarah found her sooner than later.

"Finish that circle and use the oak logs to start a fire." Fiona tapped her foot in front of the boxcar door. "Do it right here." She returned to the house and poured moon water in a basin while the other girl added herbs and salts at her direction.

The sun was already setting so there was no time for

a full ritual bath, but she did her best. She peered out of the dusty window and smiled as the girl slid a purple robe over her clothes. As she hoped, three bats gathered in the twilight at the feeder she'd hung. Fresh bats were an essential healing component for the potion she'd concocted and the only thing missing.

The nectar was laced with a slight sedative, so it was easy to snatch the bat from the feeder. She held a hatpin topped with a freshwater pearl and stabbed the bat in the chest, squeezing exactly twelve drops of its blood into the potion jar.

Then the second witch's knock came. It was so loud that it shook the little house until wooden beams began to fall from the ceiling. Having not truly contemplated death as an option until then, Fiona stood trembling for a long moment after the foundation quieted. The witch was old and tired and even if she successfully healed her cancer, she would have to do battle with Brona's children, effectively taking over Chuparosa in order to remain there. And she would remain there one way or another because returning to Vista Pines was out of the question.

She thought again of the sigils around the boxcar. If Thomas had been right about the portals, she supposed it was possible for her to leave that reality altogether and perhaps find beings on the Other Side who could increase her power and extend her life indefinitely. The opportunity was too tempting to ignore, but she would have to hurry.

* * *

Sarah parked behind the house and stifled a gasp as she took in the horrifying scene that had once been Laura's beautiful back porch. Sunlight glinted off the chunks of patio door glass they'd missed when sweeping up, shards of pottery lay everywhere with herbs and flowers drooping limply over the terra cotta tile, and what wasn't broken was scorched black.

Mena was seated on an upside-down bucket, scrubbing blood from one of the walls, and Audi delicately picked through a broken planter, uprooting a sage bush that had somehow survived the worst of it. A shiver ran up Sarah's spine as it occurred to her that she'd not only abandoned her sister to whatever happened out there but had casually sent her daughter into the danger as well.

Laura stepped around the mess to join Drew at the side of the house where he fought with an old generator that was making an unhealthy grinding noise. He showed her some things she did not understand, waving his hands at the machine while she dutifully nodded and furrowed her brow.

It was one of those strange, warm but cool desert afternoons, teasing that a break in the weather was on its way, but not there yet. Laura wore her favorite cutoff jean shorts with a thin, dark green, loose-fitting blouse that gave her a bohemian look. She'd let her hair dry naturally for the first time in decades and long copper curls fell across her collarbone as she bent to examine the damaged electrical box. Strands of white ribboned through her curls, looking as though they were there by design rather than the passing of time and it was a beautiful style for her. Laura pushed some hair behind her ears and even from that distance, Sarah could see the angry red and purple marks left around her sister's wrists by the troll's rope.

For the first time in Sarah's memory, Laura looked fragile—small even—as she moved among the enormous men taking up space on her porch. As always, it was clear that Sebastian, Chuck, and Drew loved her and wanted to take care of her, but what Sarah gathered at a glance, they would never be able to comprehend.

Laura's skin would be crawling with feelings of vulnerability and helplessness that were exposed by that troll. She was hiding her pain from them and hiding that, at the very least, she needed to lie down. Worse, Sarah knew that her stubborn sister would be hating the fact that she needed to lie down at all.

Brian jumped out of the vehicle with Becky on his heels. He ran to Laura and allowed her to make a fuss over him long enough to reassure himself of her well-being and then he broke away to help Drew with the generator.

Drew looked over his shoulder and waved to Sarah but then turned away quickly, his expression unreadable. Audi flashed her a peace sign but didn't bother to get up, let alone run to her. Sarah knew she could not be blamed for the need to process her feelings after Rueben's death, but she was beginning to feel the effects of shutting out everyone that mattered in her life to do so.

She steeled herself for whatever was to come next, followed Laura inside, and caught her tossing a handful of Ibuprofen into her mouth as if they were candy.

"I love your hair." She said, as cheerfully as possible. "Why did we ever start straightening it anyway?"

In spite of the dark circles, Laura's eyes sparkled when she rolled them and said, "Remember, Mom told us 'curly equals crazy'."

Sarah snorted. "I did not remember that. Good god, the irony."

"Look what Racine's sent over!" Mena and Audi carried in a tray full of sandwiches, several bags of chips, and a gallon jug of iced tea.

Mena handed Laura a note. It was from Molly, who worked at Racine's, and it said, "The Desert Doves will be there for you with whatever you need."

Laura smiled. "Good to know."

Sarah took plates from the cabinet, wincing at the empty spaces left by all the dead plants, and they set up a buffet in silence until Laura began to think out loud.

"I was afraid for my business, but this will change things for the better. Bash doesn't have as much desert landscaping in the back, so I won't be confined to the pots anymore."

"It's time for a lot of changes." Mena gave Sarah the side eye. "At least everyone's still in one piece."

Though she was wounded and tired, the fire behind Laura's eyes burned brighter than Sarah had seen in a long time. After surveying the damage to her body and her home, the fear she had felt earlier for her family, her life, and her future was being replaced with fury-fueled determination.

Fiona was bearing down on them and, though she hated the thought, Laura would fight her as long as it took to be free of her. Sarah was betting that soon after, the Other Side would witness the painful and permanent destruction of one Richard, the troll.

"Beck!" Bash shoved his tools at Chuck and gathered his daughter into a bear hug. When she yelped for mercy, he pulled back and took her hands, looking her over for injuries.

Becky scanned the yard and lowered her voice. "I'm alright Dad but, are you? Is everyone else? This is crazy."

Bash ran a hand through his hair. "I've always been honest with you about my life, honey. Now you've finally seen some of this shit firsthand. If you're gonna be here, it's important that you know what you're in for."

"Dad, seriously, you don't need to..."

"Yeah, you're a grown woman and I can't stop you, but you need to know all the players and all the rules."

"I can help with that." Audi approached with a seltzer water in each hand. "Mango and blackberry represent the whole of Auntie's stash, and they're kind of warm."

Bash introduced them and Becky selected the mango can. She picked at the dirt under her nails, pulled at her grubby shirt and ran a hand through her own gnarled hair. "I'm a disaster."

Audi snorted, "Have you looked around? I'll run you to the house. You're probably a size eight or so and my stuff will fit you. I'll give you all the necessary details on the way. There are lots."

"Sounds good to me." Becky popped the top off her drink, "Did you know these are great with vodka?"

"Got that at home, too. Sheriff, we'll be back later."

Bash rubbed his hand over his face. "Great."

Chuck laughed and handed him back his hammer. "Bash, I've been blown up, shot at, and stabbed. You and me, we've fought everything from vampires to angels to, well, trolls now, I guess. But having an adult child is the most stressful thing I've ever gone through." He clapped Bash on the shoulder. "That's what they don't tell you, man, because the species would end if we knew what it was like to have to let them go."

"I'm getting her back and letting her go at the same time."

"It's fucked up, but we don't expect anything different, right?"

Bash slammed a nail into the plywood. "No, I suppose not."

Chapter Eighteen

Everyone froze in the sandwich line when Brian gave Bash a slight shoulder check on his way outside. When Bash followed him, the others made a silent, collective decision to eat indoors. The timing wasn't ideal, but Bash had been waiting on that confrontation for a long time, knowing all too well the protective instincts of the son of a single mother.

Brian was a man, but his inherent mistrust of men had complicated his entire life. Bash doubted he could commit greater sins in the boy's eyes than loving or leaving his mother. The no-win situation had to be dealt with and he'd put it off for too long.

"You got something to say to me?"

Brian hadn't known what would happen when he hit the sheriff, and hadn't planned out what he would say, but he stood up tall and squared his shoulders. "I know what you did to save her, and I'm grateful. But..."

Bash glimpsed the pistol on the young man's hip that hadn't been there before and interrupted him. "You know, the list of beings that want to kill me gets longer every day. Do I need to add your name to it?" He held up a finger. "Before you answer, I'm not gonna lie. Some days your mom is at the top of that list."

Brian swallowed hard. "The only time you need to worry about me is if you break her heart. Again."

"Then, I guess we're good."

Though Bash knew it would never really be that simple, he was relieved when Brian's shoulders relaxed, and he would take the conversation for what it was—a good start.

"Christ, I wasn't gonna shoot you." Brian unconsciously pulled some electricity through his fingers. "I want to be ready for anything later on."

Bash took a bite of his sandwich and mumbled, "Is that thing still jamming?"

Laura paced through the house like a caged lion until Mena met her in the middle of the living room with a shot of whiskey.

"I don't need to take this," she said, pushing Mena's hand away.

"Honey, we need you to take it."

Laura tossed it back and waved her hand in the direction of the porch. "It's all because of me."

Drew poured himself a shot and clinked his glass against hers. "And for you, they will work it out."

When Laura could stand it no more, she peeked out the window, astonished to find Bash and Brian bent over what was left of her worktable taking Brian's gun apart.

"Can you believe this?" she said to Mena.

Mena huffed and took a shot for herself. "Suddenly best buddies like their relationship hasn't been on your late-night worry roster for months. I cannot believe men sometimes."

The group funneled out to the porch, finally dispersing some of the tense energy that had been clinging to the air in the house. As they finished their lunch, Watson laid at Laura's feet, having not let her out of his sight since his *big man* and the others brought her back to him. His legs twitched in his sleep as, in his dream, he relived his fight with the troll, watching helplessly from under the grill while his Laura screamed in pain.

Laura slid onto the tile to soothe him as he kicked and yipped. "Bash," she pulled him to the ground next to her, "Watson was next to me the day Tromluí attacked."

Sarah shook her head, "When was this?"

"The dust devil...the day I fell, when we met Richard."

Laura's exasperation with her sister was beginning to show and she snapped at her, "I texted you about that, Sarah."

Watson leapt up, facing away from them and barking at some evil they couldn't see. Laura rose to her knees and clapped her hands. "Watson! Watson, look at me!"

She reached for him, but Brian shouted, "Mom, no!"

"Hold on!" Chuck ran inside and returned with a thick towel wrapped around his forearm. He crouched by the dog and nodded to Laura. "Ok, now."

"Watson, sweet boy, it's me." she cooed.

Chuck held out his protected arm and Watson spun around, giving it a half-hearted chomp while tilting his head toward the sound of Laura's voice. He remained lightly latched on as Chuck led him closer to Laura and when they reached her, the dog's back legs buckled, and he buried his head in her neck.

"That's it, god dammit," Drew held out his hand and heaved Chuck to his feet. "Here's what we know: according to Daniel, Fiona summoned Tromluí, so it's bound to her. But according to Becky, Fiona is dying."

"Thomas convinced her that a healing ritual would work better here in Chuparosa," Sarah added, "probably with the help of the Other Side, but it's unlikely that he was able to recruit anyone over there, especially if Adira had anything to say about it. Fiona is devious, but she's physically weak, and since she relies so heavily on the spirit, I don't know how much raw power she has left."

"We know that thing can give us waking nightmares now so be hyper aware of that." Drew sighed, "In order to destroy the spirit, you might have to do something awful."

Laura turned to Sarah. "Are we ready to kill our own grandmother?"

Sarah's solemn expression turned fierce, "She put that thing on Brian and Becky without thinking twice about it, and she'd already brainwashed two other kids. The woman is cold, Laura—so cold that she can hurt Thomas's feelings."

Laura raised an eyebrow. "Hmm...useful information."

"Yeah, let's put a pin in that, just in case." Drew agreed. "I don't get why he would send her to an old train station though."

"In the seventies, the cotton farmers around here used to load their bales on the trains headed to the coast for export," Chuck explained, "but when the area outside of Chuparosa was built up, those farmers sold out and the old train yard has been abandoned for at least twenty years."

He turned to Sarah, "You're telling us that Thomas believes there's a special portal somewhere in the area. That tracks with what Daniel said, and the county sent an email last week saying they're gonna move those old railcars downtown at the end of the month."

Laura made a face. If a stable portal was on a train, the world could get larger for a lot of creatures.

"Based on Richard's ramblings, his friends are probably planning to use that portal to expand their horizons."

Drew shot a glance at the other men. "Like Daniel said at the bar, 'Imagine harpies flying over Phoenix'."

"Our wild cards are the angels and the troll," Bash added. "If any one of them shows up, we'll need to pivot fast. Stay out of that portal because we still don't know where it goes."

"And another thing: Thomas might hate Fiona, but he's not likely to help us either."

"Remember Sarah," Drew reminded her, "make sure to keep one eye open for Daniel."

"Alright," Laura said, "let's get the supplies we need, get the kids, and meet back here in two hours. Fiona's probably out there by now. She's sick, but she's got at least two girls under her spell, and we have to protect them, too."

"When Adam wakes up," Drew offered, "I'll have him head over and let us know if there's any activity on either Side."

Sarah curled her lip, "Wakes up?"

Bash shuddered, "He's a vampire."

"What?"

Sensing Laura's growing frustration, Bash added, "Just let it go, Sarah."

"No, Sebastian, What about Cara? When did this happen?"

"How dare you?" Laura's patience had finally run out. "For months I've defended you, given you space and picked up your slack. I will never regret that, but don't you come here after everything we've been through and make demands for information that you would have had if, just once, you'd answered your fucking phone."

"This is old news, Sarah, relatively speaking," Drew said carefully. "Let's focus on what's coming at us right now."

Laura stormed into the house snapping at Sarah over her shoulder, "You're going to have to stay in touch with us until this is over. If we live through it, you can do whatever you want."

Bash hung back as the rest of the group dispersed, doing his best to sound cheerful. "Was the weather nice and cool up there in Flag?"

"Not quite as chilly as it is down here." Sarah kicked at a piece of the crumbling pergola.

Bash moved close to her, but she held her hands up to stop him. She'd wanted to be left alone, and maybe she did need it at the time, but she'd ignored them and hurt them until they granted her wish. They still loved her but being put at arm's length of that love was a miserable, heartbreaking experience that she hadn't been prepared for.

"I asked for this, it's my own fault."

Bash spoke carefully, "I know what it's like to turn guilt into a wedge. It took a long time for me to learn that shutting people out doesn't make it any easier to sleep at night." He crossed his arms and leaned against the wall. "Wouldn't you rather wake up next to Drew than with a bunch of empty suffering?"

She choked back a sob and he laughed, pulling her to him. "Sarah, you're smarter than most of us—not me, of course," she pushed him away, laughing through her tears as he continued, "but if we make it through tonight, I'm sure you'll figure out how to make it through what comes next."

Adam woke an hour or so before sunset and pulled on jeans, hiking boots and a thick, hooded sweatshirt. Cara was still sleeping soundly and though she knew what he was going to do, she would have balked at his plan to get started in the sunlight, so he left her with a light kiss and a note on the nightstand. After rooting in the hall closet for a pair of gloves, he quietly closed the front door behind him.

Not willing to risk someone spotting his truck, he set out on foot to the location in Drew's text. He was not as quick as a movie vampire, *if only*, but he could move twice as fast as his friends. Right outside of town, at the base of Monitor Hill was a small broken-down building next to what the locals referred to as 'the old tracks'.

Trains still ran through the area but didn't stop at that station anymore and the old tracks were rusted and overgrown with weeds. Several boxcars had been abandoned along the old tracks as though the rail company never thought it worth the effort to move them.

At first glance, the cars appeared to be tagged heavily with graffiti, but after a closer inspection, Adam frowned. He recognized several repetitions of the sigil Drew described—the one that had been branded into the side of Laura's skull. It became clear to him that there were sigils of all kinds everywhere. They were etched in the walls and scratched in the dirt as well.

He couldn't find the old witch Drew mentioned, but from his vantage point on top of the hill, he did see two young women building a fire and pouring salt. "Close enough."

He pulled out his phone, then squinted in disbelief as several goblins exited one of the train cars.

"Well, well, well. I wonder who invited you fellows to the party."

Chapter Nineteen

"Hey, sweetheart, did you miss me?" Drew's tabby cat, Daphne, rubbed her back against Bash's legs. He picked her up and smirked at his friend.

Drew harrumphed at her and dropped a handful of shotgun shells into the pocket of his cargo pants. "I'm standing right here, you two-timer."

Unfazed, Daphne snuggled under Bash's chin until Laura walked in with Watson. The cat's contempt for the German Shepherd was matched only by her indignation at the audacity of Drew to allow the dog in the house. Bash released her under Drew's bed and left the door to his room open so she could keep track of their activities without having to socialize.

"I think we have everything we need, and the kids are on their way," Laura announced.

Drew's cell phone rang out with the first line of a Smashing Pumpkins' song.

"That's not funny," Bash grumbled.

Chuck pushed a few bullets, one by one, into his magazine. "It's a little funny, man."

Adam whispered as loud as he dared into the other end of the phone, "You're not going to believe this."

Drew rubbed at the bridge of his nose, disappointed that his headache had never really gone away, and said, "Unfortunately, I'm sure I will."

Outside, they loaded up his 4Runner and Bash's truck as the kids pulled up with Noah.

"That's the preacher? How did I not see him before?" Becky leaned over the back seat. "He's hot in like, a vintage sort of way."

"Right?" Audi gushed.

"Leave the poor man alone." Brian made a retching noise, "You're nauseating, both of you."

Noah dug through the medical bags in the back of his truck and gave the others small pouches of emergency first aid that would fit in their cargo pockets.

They were gathering the rest of their gear when Becky shrieked and froze at the sight of Laura with the biggest dog she'd ever seen. Laura took Watson by the collar, and he stood patiently waiting for Becky to decide what to do. Her father had mentioned Watson several times but, somehow, Becky never thought she'd come face to face with him.

"I'm sorry. I don't...I don't like dogs."

"He's not a dog, he's a hellhound. Totally different." Brian's tone was flippant, but he put his arm around Becky's waist and led her around Noah's pickup.

Noah and Mena stayed behind with the vehicles, about half a mile from Adam's position. They were far enough away to avoid being seen but close enough to help if anyone in the group were injured.

Staying low, the others fanned out across the hill in search of Adam. When they found him, his face was red, blotchy and peeling at his forehead.

"Adam, what happened to you?" Laura took off her bandana and tried to wrap it around his head, but he waved off her concern.

"It was a little early for me, but I'll be alright. I should have brought one of those." The group wore large bandanas around their faces in hopes that they would offer some protection if Tromluí showed up.

"Keep it," Adam told her, "the sun is almost set, and I don't dream."

"Jesus," Bash whispered to himself.

Becky peered through her binoculars into the broken window of the abandoned station house.

"Crap." She thumped Brian and guided his head to where she was looking. He nodded in agreement, so she made her way to her father. "Dad, that's her."

Laura looked through her own binoculars and watched as the old woman lit a small lantern and tucked her thick hair into a low bun on the back of her neck.

"Alright, come on Watson." She flicked her fingernails and pulled a fireball into her hand while instructing the others, "Kick through any of those cairns and sigils that you see on the ground. They're probably beacons for creatures from the Other Side and we don't need that kind of trouble right now."

She pulled Sarah along behind her, "We can't break that circle, so we'll have to draw her out."

"They haven't finished unloading," Becky took Audi's hand and they started down the hill to where Fiona's van was parked. "We'll get her attention."

Bash grabbed her shoulder. "Be careful."

She smiled at him. "Relax Dad, it's a white van. It's probably full of candy, right?"

Bash shook his head, anxiety spreading through his insides, but Brian followed the women down the hill, assuring him that he would cover them. Before Bash could protest, Chuck moved between him and Drew, pushing them even lower to the ground.

"Is that what I think it is?"

Bash racked the slide on his shotgun. "Dammit."

A harpy swooped in just out of range, shrieking, "We're the ones who aren't fucking around!"

"Look!" Drew turned their attention to two goblins emerging from one of the train cars, headed for the kids. One fell to the ground as Brian shot it then the girls made a run for the vehicle. "So much for a surprise attack on Fiona—Laura! Head's up!"

When they reached the van, the Bobs emerged from either side of it, blocking their way. Becky shrieked and covered her ears with her hands. In their minds, the girls heard small voices warning them.

"Pain."

"Pain."

"Bad."

"Bad."

Becky was breathing hard. "My dad said the mountain lion could talk but I didn't...I couldn't believe that."

"You'll probably want to revisit all of your conversations about us then." Audi put her hands as close to the van as she dared, feeling for magic. "The Bobs are usually on our side and I think they're warning us about this door."

"She put a spell on it?"

"Yeah, but it's not very strong, Fiona's either careless or clueless."

"So how do we get in?"

The Bobs herded Becky to one side of the van while Audi positioned herself at the back.

"Like this." She swept her arms in front of her and the back doors flew open. One of the bobcats jumped in and sniffed at the boxes, barring them from some and leading them to others while his brother stood guard outside.

"Ugh, this smells just like her trailer." Becky complained. "Your house didn't smell like this and neither did Laura's."

"Magic is all about intention." Audi popped open a small, wooden box. "We won't hurt anyone," she gave the contents a sniff and curled her lip, "unless they hurt us first."

The box contained several vials labeled, "Solution." She wasn't sure if the label meant it was a good thing or a bad thing but handed two of the vials to Becky and pocketed two herself.

"Let's get out of here."

"What about the rest of this stuff?" Becky asked.

Audi poked quickly through the mason jars and piles of herbs. "There is nothing she has done that I want any part of."

"What about this?" Becky pulled the lid off a banker's box full of old looking papers and books.

"Be careful, don't touch any of it." Once satisfied they weren't hexed, Audi shuffled through the papers and made a face. "This is all in some kind of secret code."

Becky grinned. "Guess what I can do?"

They put the lid back and Audi tucked the box under her arm. She hopped out and shoved the box behind a bush telling the Bobs, "If we live, I'll take this home to my mother." She knelt in front of them to make sure they understood. "If we don't live, you have to get rid of it."

"Yes."

"Yes."

"Brian! Where are you?"

He popped around from the driver's side and Audi lit a zippo, "Light this nasty thing up."

"Hang on." As the other goblin dashed around the van, Brian shoved it in, grabbed the flame and filled the inside with fire as Audi and Becky each slammed a door shut. The goblin threw itself against the walls, rocking the van violently, but soon the contents erupted into little explosions that quieted the creature and took Fiona's legacy with them.

Fiona dropped two pounds of selenite in a tote bag and carefully packed the dead bat and the potion jar on top of the crystals. In one hand she carried a poisonous powder, created in case she found it necessary to slow something down on that 'Other Side' Thomas spoke of. With the other, she gathered some fig branches from the counter and shouted to the girls, "Move it!"

A violent convulsion rocked her entire body as her magic in the van exploded. She watched in stunned disbelief from the window of the shack as flames engulfed nearly everything she'd ever worked on— every potion and spell jar catalogued over eighty years. Furious, she threw open the door, but immediately shrank away from the biggest German Shepherd she'd ever seen. The growling dog paced at the edge of her protective circle next to a copper haired woman whose hands were full of fire.

It was like looking at a long-forgotten photo of herself. The woman had to be the oldest of Brona's children and, Fiona swore under her breath, another elemental witch to boot. She would need to use extreme caution but had come too far to be intimidated by a little bit of fire.

"Who d'ya think ya are?" She lifted her chin slightly as the flame in Laura's hand grew.

"If you let those girls go, you can go home too, without any trouble. Laura made a face at the burning van. "I'll even pay for the rideshare back to Flagstaff."

She looked over her shoulder at the harpies taunting the men and shot flames into one of them.

"As you can see, I've got other things to do."

The warning was not lost on Fiona, but she wasn't ready to back down either. "I'm not goin' back to Flagstaff, and I have other things to do myself." She whispered the familiar summons for her spirit, and Laura pulled the bandana tightly around her face, spinning a fire spiral into a shield as Tromluí swept between them. Fiona swore again as it darted around the fire and moved across the desert in search of another target.

"It doesn't have to be this way." There was a brief period of time, after learning her mother had been a witch, that Laura wished they could have shared their skills with each other. Sadly, Brona was convinced that though she herself had *repented*, her daughters were abominations bound for Hell, and she had little interest in them beyond what was required by her contract with Thomas.

As if reading Laura's mind, Fiona mocked her. "Your mother had some talent but never applied herself. No matter how much I punished her, Brona was way too stubborn to learn. Had I known the angels were interested, I would have made arrangements with 'em myself."

"I didn't think it was possible, but you're worse than she ever could have been." Sarah said, appearing out of nowhere to stand next to Watson.

Laura did not know her sister had mastered invisibility but managed to hide her surprise. Fiona, on the other hand, gasped in both amazement and anger. In her stupidity, Brona had created magical beings like the world hadn't seen in ages and she was furious at having been denied access to their power.

Even so, her voice softened and her tactic changed. "Like it or not, lassies, we're family. With yer mother gone, you got no one else. Imagine what we could accomplish together."

Fiona's words sickened Laura and she finally understood where Brona's manipulative streak came from. At least her mother had given up magic completely. Having survived Fiona's abuse and having been taught to rely on potions and poisons, no wonder Brona thought it evil and depraved.

"Hello, my darlings," Thomas alit beside them and propped his elbow on Sarah's shoulder, "do you hear the banshee?" When she shook her head, he said, "That's because banshees call for loved ones, and she is nothing to you. You are certainly nothing to her."

Fiona scowled at him. "He made me summon the

nightmares so don't believe that he cares for you either."

Laura glared at Thomas. "I know what he did."

Fiona hunched over, trying to make herself look small. "I guess I'm the bad guy for trying to take care of myself. What was I supposed to do?"

"Tell him, 'No.' I do it all the time."

Pain spread down Fiona's arms and she did not think she could stand it for much longer, so she popped the top off the poison powder and blew it at Sarah.

Thomas spread his wings and stepped in front of her as the particles landed. "No one punishes my children except me." Though the flakes of poison burned him slightly, he goaded her, "Looks like you're losing your touch anyway."

Chapter Twenty

Waiting by the trucks on the other side of the hill, they could hear the gunshots and screaming harpies.

"They're in trouble," Mena worried.

Noah grabbed one of his bags. "Stay here."

"Like hell." She grabbed the other bag and scrambled up the hill behind him. They spotted Drew shuffling his feet to erase a sigil from the dirt while a harpy soared just over his head. He ducked away from the angry vulture, taunting, "Oh, sorry, did you need that?"

Mena slapped her hands to her mouth as Chuck hollered, "Get down!" and shot it out of the sky.

Adam called to Bash after counting at least nine more circling harpies, "We've got to find that portal and close it down or they'll keep coming."

Bash kicked over a cairn as they ran toward the abandoned boxcars, then stopped to pick up one of the rocks, showing Adam how it glowed in his hand. "These are just like the ones we saw on the Other Side."

Two goblins stood guard near the car that was covered with the most magical graffiti. "That must be the place." Adam said.

Bash reloaded his shotgun and racked the slide, grinning to himself. "Did you know I met Laura on a goblin hunt?"

"That's one of the most fucked up things I've ever heard."

"You turned Cara into a vampire."

Adam rubbed his chin. "I suppose you've got me there."

Bash shot one of the goblins and tried not to throw up as Adam pulled the other one apart with his bare hands. "Well, none of us were ever gonna be romantic heroes."

Adam disagreed but, as he opened his mouth to respond, his face contorted with pain. Bash fell backward in shock as a splintered wooden beam tore through the vampire's chest. A goblin they hadn't noticed before had staked him as it leapt out of the train car. Bash shot it as it tried to escape, but Adam still slumped to the ground.

"Christ, Adam." Bash fell on his knees beside him. "Don't pull it, you'll bleed out."

Adam grasped frantically at the stake, using both hands to pull it through as much as he could.

"Get it...get it out of me...now Sebastian," He screamed, "Don't think about it, just do it."

Bash took hold of the stake and yanked it all the way through, then tossed it away and pushed his hands into the wound. "There's so much blood, I can't stop it."

Adam let his head fall backward. "There's nothing you can do."

Bash knew better, and his mouth went dry just thinking about it. Even so, he said, "There is...I know there is."

"No, I won't do that. I told you that I'll never hurt you." Bash pushed up his sleeve and brought his forearm to Adam's mouth.

Adam pushed him away, but Bash set his jaw and shoved his arm forward again, "You better do it now before I...before I just can't."

Adam gradually lowered his fangs, but when he tried to pull Bash's arm to his mouth, his bite was stopped by Laura's shield bracelet.

Bash whispered into the air, "Woman, I love you," then unclipped the bracelet and let it fall into the sand.

"I'm...sorry." By that time, Adam was gasping for every breath.

His chest tightened with fear, and Bash growled, "Shut up and do it now, dammit."

Before Bash could finish his sentence, Adam's fangs sank into his vein. The sudden shock of pain caused his vision to tunnel, then his hand began to tingle and burn. Panicking, he grabbed a handful of Adam's hair, ready to rip himself away, but Adam's grip on his arm was so tight that he was unsure if he could. Digging deep into his soul for courage, he did his best to hold his arm still instead.

Sebastian's blood flowed steadily, enabled by the thundering of his terrified heart. It had the woodsy taste of juniper berries that Adam found intoxicating and though Bash fell forward, groaning from the pain, Adam couldn't help pulling his arm tighter against his mouth.

It took little more than a minute for Adam's wound to close and for Bash to feel him loosen his grip. He was dizzy and cold and couldn't believe it when he heard himself ask, "Is that gonna be enough?"

Adam wiped his chin with the back of his hand and took Bash by the shoulders, gently leaning him against the boxcar steps. He tore off the bottom of his shirt and tied it around the swollen holes in Bash's arm, holding pressure as tightly as he could without breaking the bone.

Bash mumbled, "You didn't kill me," and tried to stand. He was a bit incoherent and, fearing he would pass out, Adam bit down on his finger and let a few drops of blood drip onto Bash's lips. It was a trick he didn't use often, but he figured if he could do it for the dog, he could do it for the brave man who'd just saved his life.

A few seconds later, Bash blinked his eyes and scrambled backward. "What did you do to me?"

"Nothing," Adam lied. He plucked up the shield bracelet. "Here, you better not lose this."

Bash clipped it to his wrist and they poked their heads around the car, learning that the harpies still hovered over Chuck and Drew, Laura and Sarah were confronting Fiona with Thomas in front of the other boxcar, and that they couldn't even see the kids.

Startled by a clamoring from above, Bash drew his pistol as six black crows flew at them, giving cover for Richard, who jumped over their heads and out of the boxcar.

Bash turned to Adam, "Are you sure you're good because this operation has gone sideways from the start and we have got to get our shit together."

Adam bared his teeth. "I'm good."

Through all the commotion, the first college girl had continued her work on the fire in front of the station house. Her supply of white oak was exhausted and she'd been dragging broken wooden furniture from the station, building a bonfire that was now over their heads.

"Stupid girl!" Hope of completing her healing spell was lost, but Fiona had not forgotten about the portal to the Other Side. Keeping the spell jar, she dropped the bag and made a break for the boxcar, shoving the girl in front of the others and shouting, "You better stop them!"

The bewildered girl lifted a burning table leg out of the fire and swung it at Laura.

"Oh, honey, don't threaten me with a good time." Laura pulled all the fire away from the girl and hurled it in front of the boxcar, blocking Fiona's escape.

Sarah raised her arms and the girl was dragged backward through the salt line in the dirt and tossed through the station's rotten siding. She had been careful, using less force to toss the girl than she'd used on Drew, but still the girl collapsed, unconscious in the rubble.

"Damn—I still can't get that right." She ran through the circle and called to her daughter to get help, but Audi was already texting Noah when she and Becky charged around the corner.

Sarah stood at Laura's side, watching as Fiona became increasingly hysterical. Her plans disintegrated in front of her, and she could not handle losing control of her situation.

"You are wicked women!" she screamed. Though it was designed to heal, Fiona altered her intention and, with genuine hatred in her heart, heaved the spell jar at Laura. "I curse you and all those you love!"

Audi snickered to Noah, "Boy, is she late to that party."

The bun she secured earlier had come loose and Fiona snatched out fistfuls of her hair when Laura engulfed the jar in flames and Sarah waved it away.

The witch's third and final death knock echoed through the desert, shaking the earth beneath them and knocking everyone to their knees. Though her body was wracked with pain, Fiona still could not believe her time was over. The crows chased her as she stumbled toward the hillside, screaming and waving her arms at the birds as she climbed.

Halfway up, the pebbles under her feet began to roll like ball bearings and she slid wildly, tumbling forward and cracking her skull against the rocks at the base of the hill.

Laura and Sarah were too stunned to move or even speak, but Noah ran to the old woman, thinking she might still be alive.

"Noah, no!" Audi cried.

They sprinted to Fiona's body but got there just as Noah was feeling for a pulse. Audi hauled him back and he fell against her, convulsing.

Laura rested her hand on his forehead and spoke softly, "Just give it a minute Noah, and you'll be okay."

Becky took one of his hands in hers, "What's wrong with him?"

"This can happen when normal people get too close to pure evil," Audi said, kissing his cheek, "it sucks but from now on, he'll be able to recognize it when he sees it."

Becky thought for a moment and then grabbed up Fiona's wrist, holding tight while her psyche endured wave after wave of frightful disquiet and dread.

Laura gaped at her and then asked her sister, "What is it about their generation?"

Sarah shook her head and returned to the station house to inspect what Fiona had left behind. She tipped the dead bat out of the cloth bag, gagging a bit as it thumped on the ground. Her intent had been to destroy her grandmother's belongings so no one else was hurt, but she smiled down at the piles of crystals and formed a new plan. She wrapped the handles of the bag closed and looked around for a rock large enough to smash it with.

Holding the rock over her head, she paused. "What do you want?"

Thomas leaned against the wall, gawking at the various creatures moving in for a second attack.

"This family will never win awards for its battle strategy, and frankly, it's embarrassing."

She thought about throwing the rock at him but changed her mind. "Get over here and make yourself useful."

He poked his head inside the bag and eyed her quizzically. "Are you sure you don't want to save all of this to help heal whoever's left in the morning?"

"Just do it, please."

He glared into the bag again and the crystals shattered into hundreds of smaller pieces.

"Selenite is a healer, but do you know what else it works on?" She lifted her chin. "Bad dreams."

"You can't kill a spirit."

"Then I'll do whatever it takes to stop it." She turned around and found herself face to face with Daniel.

He unfurled his wings, reached out and grabbed her by the throat. "So will I, Sarah."

Chapter Twenty-One

Sarah pulled at Daniel's hands and pushed his wings away with her magic but could not break free.

"You don't understand..." she rasped.

His grip tightened around her throat. "Time after time, with my own eyes, I've watched you shamelessly colluding with Thomas."

Thomas unfurled his wings as well. "Let her go." His voice was no longer haughty, but hard. "Tonight, Daniel, you would be wise to accept all the help you can get."

Sarah focused her intention on the smokey quartz that hung at her throat. It pulsed with a faint glow and Daniel was briefly blinded as the light from the crystal surged and flowed around her body in a protective aura.

He released her throat, catching her around the waist as she fell forward, fighting for breath. He pulled a dagger from his belt as Thomas advanced on him.

"Why are you doing this? Fiona is gone."

Though her crystal still offered some protection, Daniel pressed the dagger to her collar bone.

"She is an abomination."

Thomas flew at him. "She is your family."

Rising to avert the attack, Daniel took Sarah with him, now kicking and screaming.

In his peripheral vision, Drew mistook Daniel's wings for a harpy and swung his shotgun around. Hearing Sarah's screams, he hesitated just in time, shouting, "Daniel, no! Please!"

Thomas took advantage of the distraction and dove at Daniel, knocking him backward and loosening his hold on Sarah.

As she fell away, Thomas shoved Daniel again. "You see everything, but you see nothing!"

Daniel swiped at him with the dagger, slashing through his wing and across his bicep, sending feathers raining down below. "After all of my warnings, I see one of my Defenses in league with the fallen."

"She uncovered Fiona's plot and saved the cowboy's daughter," Thomas jerked backward as Daniel lunged for him again. "Even knowing I lured her there, she saved me, too."

"Their only job is to stop those who would take the earth from the humans and you are corrupting them with your own obsessions."

Thomas shook Daniel by the shoulders. "Look around, brother, the script is everywhere. You must know that it's not just me who wants to be free. The creatures from the old days are simply riding its coat tails. This is bigger than us and you will get all of your Defenses killed if you don't open your eyes."

Daniel tore away from him, shaking his head furiously. "They were destroyed and there are no more."

"It's using that imbecile of a troll as a scout and that spell does much more than open a gate."

"How can you know this?"

"I know because, centuries ago, I taught them how to do it."

Daniel's eyes flared with rage and he rushed at Thomas, shoving him against the hill.

Thomas had not intended to fight his brother that day, but if Daniel couldn't see beyond his occupation to the bigger threats at play, he was prepared to do anything to stop him. He felt Daniel's dagger sink into his side, but he pushed back, and they rolled, fighting and thrashing their wings.

Thomas was beginning to understand why his escape from Hell was not thwarted and that his children were more important than he ever imagined. While he cared nothing about who walked the earth or why, Lucifer had no doubt been watching their struggles with something much more than amusement. Beings much viler than their master were chained in Hell, just waiting for their moment while the likes of Daniel denied the coming upheaval and eliminated their best chances for survival.

Thomas wriggled out of Daniel's grasp and let himself slide until his body collided against the boots of someone poised halfway down the hill. The light from a silver circlet on their brother's head shone so brightly that Thomas could see nothing else.

Using his arm to shield his eyes, he rose to his knees and whispered, "Michael."

The light from Michael's halo dimmed and from a sheath on his hip, he drew a short sword and placed it under Thomas's chin.

Daniel alit next to them bowing his head, "Dream Master."

Michael glowered at them both in disgust. "Where is the spirit?"

Drew dove to cushion the blow as Sarah fell to the ground, but then roughly shoved her away just before being engulfed by the familiar whirlwind of crystal dust.

When Tromluí withdrew, she crawled to him. "What's going to happen to you?"

Demoralized by what he knew was coming, he slumped against her, and though wide awake in the heat of the desert, a coolness rushed over his skin. Squinting through the bloody water, he heard Sarah calling, but could only strike against the walls of the baptismal pool.

"Drew!" she tried to shake him out of it and then tried to hold him, but he convulsed so hard that the best she could do was rest his body gently on the ground.

Sarah dumped the bag of selenite and used her mind to make a whirlwind out of the crystal crumbs, blending it into the particles of Tromluí. The spirit squealed and separated and flew about until finally it calmed, swirling low to the ground, weak and confused and unsure of where to go.

She'd stopped it, but was too late to help Drew, who broke her heart with his unintelligible screams.

Hearing their cries, Daniel turned on Thomas again. "Thanks to you, they were losing this battle before it ever began."

The three of them flew to the struggling Defenses and Michael lifted Andrew to his feet. As the Dream Master worked magic on the terrified preacher, Thomas looked around and noticed Adam and Bash attempting to engage the troll as Richard moved from one boxcar to another. They were waylaid by his goblin guards and though Thomas was weakened, he slunk around the commotion and followed closely as Richard vaulted up the ladder of one of the cars.

Thomas was bleeding, with filthy, broken wings, but leaned casually against the door as if he'd come straight from Heaven. "I have a few questions for you, Dick."

The troll whirled around and sneered when he recognized Thomas. "You think you can take this world from us and then invade the Other Side, too?"

Thomas peered at him. "Have you done something different with your hair?"

Richard's hair had, in fact, been falling out in clumps since he'd taken Laura and there were bald patches emerging all over his head. Rather than comment, he eyed the wounds Thomas incurred during his fight with Daniel.

"You have no friends at all—not even your own kind."

Thomas filled his hands with electricity, "Next question: who said you could leave your post at the bridge?" He ran his fingers over the spell work on the walls. "I know you're not this smart. You can barely speak your own language, let alone mine. Who taught you these words?"

"The Other Side is too small for some of us."

"And you think that with portals on the trains, you can just ride around, exploring what's over here? Is it your plan to race home if things in the city go 'sideways', as the cowboy says?" He clucked his tongue. "You won't like the big city, Dick."

"Humans will learn to fear us."

Thomas threw his head back and laughed. "Do you know what humans do to things they're afraid of? I don't really care what happens to you, though. I want to know who taught you that spell."

"Your master cannot keep us locked up anymore."

Thomas shrugged. "It's okay, I'll figure it out, but the next question does require an answer." He sent a funnel of electricity into Richard's chest. "What made you think you could go after my daughter?"

Richard leered toward the door, in Laura's direction. "She will help us, or she will be my prize." Thomas increased the flow of power, and Richard rushed him.

Outside, Laura saw the lightning and heard them crashing around. She climbed the ladder to find Richard had managed to get Thomas chest to chest on the ground.

"Hey, now." She repeated Richard's favorite phrase and threw a fireball from the doorway. He released Thomas and surged forward to grab her, but she leaned off the steps, holding tight to the railing as Watson leapt through the door and latched his teeth onto Richard's shoulder. He wrestled loose and the dog landed unconscious near where Thomas lay powerless on the floor.

Richard dragged her through the doorway and threw her against the wall, snarling, "You did this to me!"

One corner of her mouth turned up when her eyes adjusted to the dimness. In his cave, she'd hexed Richard to be as hideous as he was arrogant. Infected sores pocked his face and the inflamed skin appeared to be flaking off in sheets. She blew on the matted clumps of his hair and mocked him, telling Thomas, "I guess my powers do work on the Other Side."

Thomas rolled up to all fours. "Laura, get out. You're still not strong enough to kill him."

Her lips thinned. "Parenting 101, Thomas. Children need encouragement."

Richard jerked her up and shook her by the shoulders. As her head fell backward, she closed her eyes and repeated the words Fiona had used to summon Tromluí.

Untethered from Fiona, and damaged by Sarah, the nightmare spirit had been slinking through the area in a low dust cloud. After hearing Laura's call, it swooped around Bash as he climbed the ladder to the boxcar. Adam pulled him down to safety and reached through the swirling particles, grabbing hold of the spirit. He squeezed his fist around its slender body, growling, "I see you."

"How did you do that?" Bash grabbed Adam's shoulder. "Why did you do that? It will be awful."

Adam's squeezed harder. "I told you, I don't dream."

Its new mistress repeated her call, and Tromluí slithered free from Adam's grasp, gathering sand and rocks as it whipped through the doors.

Richard grabbed Laura's chin. "This is familiar." He turned her face to the south wall and though it was hard to see at first, the gateway soon became clear, pulsing with energy.

She twisted in Richard's grasp, giving the spirit space to wrap itself around his head. He blinked his eyes furiously and threw her to the floor. Anxious to please Laura, Tromluí used all of the strength it had left to turn the boxcar, in Richard's mind, into the stones of a bridge that crumbled on top of him.

She rubbed her hands together, then flicked her fingernails, throwing stream after stream of static wrapped fire at Richard's torso. He stumbled toward her, roaring for more goblins.

Bash popped his head over the threshold, and she stopped him, waving at Thomas and yelling, "Get him out of here!"

Bash dragged Thomas to the doorway and pushed him out to Adam, who waited below. He shouted, "Blow the other boxcars!" And disappeared inside.

Laura extended her hands and pulled in the entire firepit that the college girl had prepared and dumped it on the troll. Bash found an iron rail spike and dug it into the wall around the portal. The portal contracted slightly, and the goblins were unable to pass through the iron.

His lungs filled with smoke, causing his head to swim with dizziness, but he followed the glimmering sigils on the walls, hoping to scratch out as many as he could before the smoke overtook him.

Unable to keep Tromluí's visions out of his head, Richard gathered himself up and swung wildly in every direction until he managed to knock Laura off her feet. She scrambled away from his grasp, so tired that she wasn't sure she could find the strength to get back up. On the other side of the boxcar, Watson woke and searched through the haze until he found his Laura slumped against a wall.

He nudged his *big man* in the knees, nearly knocking him down to get his attention, and as Bash helped Laura to her feet, Watson brought her a burning oak branch from the fire.

"Richard!" She called out, and when the troll moved toward the sound of her voice, she swung the branch, hitting him squarely on the side of the head. As he fell backward, Watson bit down on his inner thigh. He then bit into every part of him that wasn't on fire and when Richard finally stilled, Bash had to pull Watson away to make him stop.

Laura calmed the flames slightly and took Richard's arms, dragging him toward the portal. Bash took his legs and together they shoved the troll's dead body through the gate. "Baby, what are we doing?"

She gave him a grim look. "We're sending a message."

Adam dropped Thomas in a heap at the door of the station house and left to find the others. The angel watched for a while as the crows menaced the bobcats, who leapt about, plucking them out of the air one by one. Assessing the damage done to him by Daniel and the troll, he concluded that it wouldn't be pretty, but he would live.

Arrogance was a trait that Thomas had nearly mastered over the years and though he wasn't likely to give his personality a total makeover, he noted ruefully that it wasn't doing him any favors.

Audi and Becky were in the station house picking through the items Fiona had left behind, so he gathered his composure and called out to them, "Excuse me, girls, Grandpa Tommy's here to babysit, and today we're going to learn how to make a bomb."

They gave each other sideways looks but when Thomas explained the plan, they searched every jar for alcohol, delighted to learn that Fiona's preservative of choice was vodka.

Adam found Chuck and Brian fighting hand-to-hand with three goblins that had dropped down on them from the top of a boxcar. Adam snatched one off its feet, squeezing his hand around its neck until the head came off and hit the ground with a sickening plunk. "I intensely dislike those creatures."

"Uh, you're not kidding, man." Chuck's shotgun was knocked from his hands when the goblins attacked, so he took advantage of the distraction and seized it up to shoot the other two. A familiar screech echoed from the harpies circling above and Brian sank against the boxcar in frustration.

"Guys, we've got to get higher, or we'll never take those things down."

Adam looked from Chuck and Brian to the boxcar. "Let's do it then."

They gathered by the broken ladder and Chuck shook his head. "This is a terrible idea."

Adam cupped his hands, "Just grab the outer railing when you land." Chuck stepped up and Adam used his vampire strength to boost him to the top of the car. He nearly skidded all the way off the other side of it, but like Adam said, he was able to grab the railing just in time to stop himself.

Brian landed in a superhero pose when Adam hoisted him up and was disappointed that no one had seen, but they were able to take down two harpies right away from their new vantage point. "Yeah, this is much better."

Adam called to Thomas, "Did they find anything?"

The girls were busy at the counter soaking strips of cloth to stuff in the jars. "Careful." Audi warned, "We don't know what she planned to do with this stuff."

As the last harpy fell, Chuck and Brian slid carefully down the railing and jumped to the ground where Adam waited.

"My knees are gonna ache for days after this, man." Chuck complained.

"Here," Adam handed him one of the makeshift bombs, "you'll feel better when you blow something up."

"Everybody, get down!" Chuck ordered.

Brian grabbed some flames from the burning van and Michael wrapped his wings around Sarah and Drew to protect them from the coming blasts.

Brian shot the fire into the boxcar as Chuck lobbed a bomb from each hand, and then Adam threw both men out of the way as the car exploded.

At the same time, Becky tossed a bomb to Bash. "Dad, catch!"

She and Audi pulled Thomas to safety, then Laura lit the bottle and Bash threw it in the portal. He grabbed Laura's hand, and with Watson between them, they jumped out of the boxcar as it blew apart.

Chapter Twenty-Two

"Is everyone okay?" Chuck counted them off with relief as each of his friends slowly lifted their heads. The boxcars were reduced to metal wheels and the station house was burning down, but it seemed that they had all survived, including Tromluí, who swirled around until it found Laura sitting on the ground with Watson, patting tiny embers out of his fur.

"How does it feel to be unhinged?" she asked it.

Laura hadn't seen Michael before and scrambled backward when he held his hands out to her. He wore camouflage cargo pants, a black t-shirt, and dusty, weathered combat boots that were caked in old blood. His hair was short, wavy, and black like his brothers', though unlike them, he had olive skin and dark eyes.

Bash noted that his uniform was of no particular country, but he was heavily armored in a vest that closed around his ribcage with straps. "Angels wear Kevlar?"

Michael smiled and shook his head, turning his attention to Laura and Tromluí. She waved her hand over the spirit. "What am I supposed to do with this thing?"

"What is your intention, Laura?"

Michael held out a satin bag and she focused, releasing Tromluí to his custody. His halo then glowed so brightly that they had to turn away and when the light was gone, so was he.

Becky flicked some rocks out of Thomas's wings. "How come you don't have one of those?"

He glared at Bash. "This is your spawn?" Bash took Becky by the arm and moved her away from Thomas, who added, "How unsurprising."

Drew looked around. "Didn't Fiona have two girls with her?"

Chuck swore. "Let's fan out."

Audi and Becky found the girl crouching behind the station house and shouted for the others. Becky stuck her hand out to help her up, but instead of taking it, the terrified girl tackled her.

"Oh, shit!" Audi jumped in to pull them apart, but Daniel stepped around her and touched the girl's forehead. Brian caught her as she collapsed into a deep sleep and carried her to where Mena and Noah waited with Fiona's other victim.

"Crap," Becky moaned. I think she broke one of my ribs."

Seeing the blood, Bash panicked. "Hold still."

"Wait, wait." she lifted her shirt and felt around for the underwire that had broken through from her bra. It poked into her skin, leaving bloody knicks across her upper torso. "False alarm."

Bash put his head in his hands and Audi laughed, "You gotta wear a sports bra when you're with us."

The others cornered Daniel at the door of the burning station house. They each had something to say to him, but Laura was the only one to speak out loud. "I thought your job was to police this family for those who are misusing their power."

"It is."

"You would kill my sister, but never thought once about stepping in to stop Fiona?"

"That's not how it works, Laura."

"Fuck how it works, Daniel."

Sarah held back as the others left to regroup away from the angel's presence, still unsure of her status with them. "If you're going to kill me," she said, without looking at him, "just do it."

"Your sister has a point," He spoke to her as if he'd just learned a secret, "I was doing my job Sarah, but I wasn't really doing the work. Your loved ones gave you space to heal and, unlike me, they never doubted you."

"It's not that simple." Sarah's eyes brimmed with tears. "I'm doing better, and I'm glad I went north, but now I have to deal with how I hurt them." She watched Audi laughing and reliving stories from the night with her peers who, as always, kept a cool distance from the others as if aging was contagious. "I guess there's no time like the present to start my apology tour."

As she walked toward her daughter he said, "It's probably not necessary, you know."

"Not to them, but it is to me."

After rescuing Laura from the Other Side, Drew decided to make arrangements with the Sheriff's stable manager to exercise Stranger a few times a week.

Though it made perfect sense, he hadn't known that Chuck and Sebastian made horseback riding part of their weekly routine, patrolling the more remote mountain areas for the lost and the injured and for those who were up to no good.

After a couple weeks of practice, the deputies started inviting him along on their patrols. He'd ridden out with them that day to follow up on the report of a badly twisted ankle in Mesquite Canyon. When they found him, the hiker was adamant that they not call a helicopter. Those rescues tended to be insanely expensive, and they usually made the nightly news.

Though it turned out that his ankle was actually broken, they were able to get the young man out on horseback and Drew had only just returned when Sarah knocked on his door.

The days were getting cooler, but beads of sweat dotted her forehead as she shifted nervously from foot to foot on his new welcome mat. It said, "Definitely Not a Trap Door." The joke made her laugh, but she stepped off the mat anyway because in Chuparosa one could never be sure—not even the owner of the house.

He didn't answer, but the 4Runner was in the driveway. Even if he didn't want to see her, it was unlike him to avoid a confrontation, though she was hoping for something much nicer than that. It took some time to muster the courage, but she allowed herself to knock once more, and when he didn't answer then, she heaved a dejected sigh and turned to leave.

"Sarah?" The door swung open behind her, and she had to steady her nerves with a hand against the wall.

He was enjoying a long, cool shower when she first knocked but had stepped out just in time for the second one. He'd pulled on some faded jeans and a t-shirt and was still holding a towel to his head when he opened the door. Her breath caught in her throat at the sight of him, but he smiled warmly and tossed the towel away to hold her hands in his.

She hesitated for a second and then blurted, "I just want to say one thing and you can send me away if you want, but I'm not going to hold back my feelings anymore."

He shook his head, "I won't make it that easy for you."

She had expected as much, but he didn't mean that the way that she thought he did. Sensing her disappointment, he led her inside, clarifying, "I'll wait for you, Sarah, I'll fight for you, and I'll love you until I die, but I will never send you away."

Her shoulders relaxed away from her ears, and she admitted, "That actually does make it easy on me." She looked up at him and said simply, "I hate that I hurt you Andrew. I've loved you since we met. I don't know how to make us happen though. I mean, we've been through so much already. Where do we even start?"

He closed his eyes to let her words sink in. After waiting for what seemed an eternity for her to come to him, he would not waste a single second more without her love in his life. He took her face in his hands. "We start with a kiss."

She melted into him, making a soft noise when his tongue found hers. He, too, was done holding back and he wrapped her in his arms, his grip tight as he kissed her with all the passion that had been building in him for years.

She slid her hands underneath his shirt and, instead of flinching away, he pulled their hips together, letting himself enjoy the sensation of her fingers as they explored his bare skin.

Feeling him hard against her was exciting, but it made her a little nervous as she wasn't used to eliciting a sexual response from a man. Drew's intensity was exactly what she craved but it occurred to her that she might need a running start. Easing him backward onto the couch, she knelt on the floor between his legs and asked, "When was the last time someone did something just for you?"

"Hmm?" She pressed her hands up his thighs, and all he could manage as she played with the rips in his jeans was a shrug and a lopsided smile.

She took her time unfastening each button and rained soft kisses across his belly as she released him from the denim. Then she wrapped her hand around him, sliding it up and down, following with her tongue and then her lips.

His head fell back, and his hands played with her hair as she moved. He'd wanted her for so long and her mouth was so soft that he thought she might drive him insane. "Sarah, honey, I'm gonna..." He arched his hips and gripped the arm of the couch. "Oh, god."

Afterward, she crawled next to him and draped her legs across his thighs. He pulled her close and laid her head against his shoulder. "Stay with me for a while. Let me impress you with dinner from my vast collection of frozen foods."

She smiled and pulled out her phone. "First, I need to let them know where I am."

"Of course." He could not suppress a boyish grin while watching her text Audi and Laura that she would be spending the night with him.

Bash hung up his phone and sat back on his heels. "Chuck says Fiona's girls are back in Flagstaff. The Desert Doves made sure they don't remember much of anything, and it sound like they'll be fine."

"That's good news." Laura wiped the sweat from her forehead, leaving a dirt smear over one eyebrow.

They'd been working in the back yard and since Bash had never tried to grow a single plant, he couldn't believe how quickly she was turning his house—their house—into a thriving botanical garden.

Pleased with their progress, she announced, "I think the rosemary will be very happy in this spot."

He kept his eyes on the trowel he dragged through the dirt, and asked, "What about you?"

She pulled off her gloves and traced a finger along his jaw. "Very happy as well."

"Good." He pressed her hand to his mouth and stood up with a loud groan, overly exaggerating an old man's walk.

"I can buy us some of those puffy gardening mats if you like." She giggled.

He stood up straight. "Don't you dare."

She reached for her back pocket and then turned her phone screen so he could read an incoming text from Sarah. "Yes!" He made a fist in the air. "It's about damn time."

As they put away the tools, she caught him scratching at the wounds left by Adam's fangs on his forearm. She touched the skin around them and tilted her head to examine his expression. He was healing remarkably well, but she was worried. In spite of her spell and Tromluí's capture, his nightmares hadn't ceased.

He kissed her forehead and dismissed her anxious look with, "I'm alright, baby," and went inside to shower.

She thought for a while about how they were adjusting to the new living arrangements. Having both been single for so long, they continued to stumble a bit over personal space and dumb things like his inexplicable attachment to the hideous rug in the guest room.

More often though, they were learning fun things about each other. In the past, they both kept music playing in their homes to combat loneliness and found that they spent a fair amount of time quietly enjoying each other's company with a soundtrack playing in the background. It was no lie when she said, 'very happy', and she would do everything in her power to make sure he was, indeed, 'alright'.

She showered after him and then puttered in the house for a while, putting a few more things away. After setting the tin man on the windowsill over the kitchen sink, she found Bash lying on the couch with a book. During his free time, he would usually be reading or watching baseball.

"Hey handsome, is there any room for me?"

He grinned and reached for her, "Hell yeah there is."

She snuggled into his arms, and he ran his fingers through her curls. They gossiped some more about Sarah and Drew, and eventually dropped off to sleep.

While they napped, Watson paced in front of the narrow window next to the front door, keeping a close eye on Daniel and Michael who peered in from the front porch.

Daniel pressed his hand against the glass to calm the dog and said, "This group of Defenses flails about when separated, but their bond seems to grow stronger with each challenge they face."

Michael was unconvinced of their motivation. "The moment our mission falls out of alignment with their so-called values, they will abandon us. They don't care who lives on the earth, only about each other."

"Yes," Daniel said thoughtfully, "but I've seen enough to believe that they're very likely to sacrifice themselves. Not for us of course, but they understand what's at stake. Moreover, if Thomas is correct, everything is converging and the one who made the amulet for the troll will come looking for the Deanes. At this point, they have no choice but to stay in the fight."

"There's work to do in the meantime." Michael reached for the door. "Thomas did not return to Hell and they have to find him before matters are further complicated."

Daniel moved in front of him. "They like us to knock." Ignoring Michael's incredulous look, he added, "I would sooner invite Thomas to lunch than interrupt them right now."

"It's just a nap."

"We have no way to reward them, so I will not take away their few moments of peace."

"Do you know what you're doing, Daniel?"

He pulled out the stone Laura had abandoned, hung it on the door handle and guided Michael away from the house.

"I'm paying my dues."

There would be no funeral for Fiona Deane. Her granddaughters buried her ashes at the foot of the hill where she died, and it was known forever after that the place was cursed.

Up in Flagstaff, Brian and Becky chatted with the amiable man who ran the market at the Vista Pines trailer park. In fact, he was so cheerful and friendly that they felt guilty deceiving him. He shared with them that his luck had changed during the past few weeks and that he was feeling better than he could ever remember feeling. Pretending to be newlyweds in search of an inexpensive home, they asked to tour the only available trailer in the park.

"I used to rent it to an older woman, but she disappeared on me...you know how it goes." Recalling how much money he'd lost on Fiona; he eyed the young couple with a bit of suspicion.

Becky put her arm in Brian's for affect and laid her head on his shoulder. "Smell the pines..." She cooed.

The manager relaxed and smiled at them. "It will take a lot to make the place livable again, but if you're willing to do the work, I can give you a discount.

The energy in the tiny trailer was stale and black and Brian choked on it when they walked in. His eyes hunted for scorpions, but the only thing on the floor was the rug Sarah and Becky used to put out the fire. It still lay charred in a heap next to the overturned couch. The stench of smoke and rot hung in the air with another smell they couldn't quite place.

The manager eyed the couple once more, but with worry. "Are you sure about this?"

"Can we look around a bit? I'm pretty handy, so maybe I can make something of it." Brian tried his best to keep a light tone.

"Sure, take your time. I'll leave you two alone to talk it over—just drop off the key before you leave." In truth, the manager felt he couldn't get out of the trailer fast enough.

They put on gloves and masks as soon as he shut the door and set about opening all the cabinets and drawers.

"We're looking for spell jars, powders, teas, dolls...anything suspicious that might hurt someone." Brian said, gagging as he picked through a drawer full of molded herbs. If not for the risk of starting a forest fire, he would have burned the entire trailer to the ground.

"Hey honey, look at this." Becky called to him from the bedroom, and he found her standing over what looked like a fish tank.

"The manager's gone so you don't have to call me honey anymore."

She gaped at him. "Alright, grumpy. But I found the smell."

Dozens of frogs climbed over each other in the tank and Brian gagged again. "Jesus."

Several trinket boxes topped the dresser, so Becky unfurled a reusable tote from her back pocket and piled them in. Brian added the molded herb packets and then a few jars from the bathroom.

"We'll burn it all later. The rest of it must have been in the van."

Becky held it away from her. "Good, because what's in this bag gives off terrible vibes."

They lit sage wands from Laura's garden and gave the place another walkthrough. An internet search told them the frogs were local, so they emptied the tank in the forest before locking up.

The manager was so relieved that they had decided not to rent the place that he gave them free sodas from the cooler for their trip home.

They loitered for a while in the tiny parking lot, enjoying the fresh air and then Brian pulled out his phone to order a ride share. "Let's get the fuck out of here."

"Hey grumpy," she touched his arm, "are you good?"

He stared for a long minute at the trailer, then leaned against a broken-down sedan. "That woman was my family. Fiona and Brona and Thomas...they are my family." He shuddered, "Drew's wrong. I'm definitely part monster."

"Your family is Laura, Sarah, Audi, my dad, the preacher and...me." She flicked a blackened piece of sage out of his hair. "You're the one who has it wrong, Brian. You're not part monster, you're part angel."

Inside the sedan, Special Inspector Samuel Parker lay hidden under a ratty blanket in the back seat. For years, he'd tried to stop Fiona Deane, but the witch had evaded his investigations every time. He had come to the trailer park as soon as he heard she was dead to do exactly what the kids had done—scuttle the place to protect the innocent.

Studying her family line was a hobby of his and it went all the way back to Kinsale, in Ireland. That was the first he'd heard of a Thomas though. The rest of the Deanes managed to contain their troubles in Chuparosa, but maybe it was time to visit their little town and say hello to his former partner, Sebastian Scott.

About the Author

Vanessa Haney grew up in rural Arizona with, tragically, no access to the Other Side. Had there been a portal, she would have gone through it a long time ago. Instead, she makes a happy life in less rural Arizona with her son Connor, her partner Mike and two black cats named Shadow and Felix. There she writes, hikes and watches way too many horror movies.

Sign up to follow her adventures at:
http://www.vanessahaneywrites.com